GROSSET & DUNLAP
Published by the Penguin Group
Penguin Group (USA) LLC, 375 Hudson Street, New York, New York 10014, USA

USA | Canada | UK | Ireland | Australia | New Zealand | India | South Africa | China

penguin.com
A Penguin Random House Company

Text copyright © 2014 by Ann Hood. Art copyright © 2014 by Denis Zilber. All rights reserved. Published by Grosset & Dunlap,
a division of Penguin Young Readers Group, 345 Hudson Street, New York, New York 10014.
GROSSET & DUNLAP is a trademark of Penguin Group (USA) LLC.
Printed in the USA.

Library of Congress Cataloging-in-Publication Data is available.

Design by Giuseppe Castellano.
Map illustration by Giuseppe Castellano and © 2013 by Penguin Group (USA) LLC.

ISBN 978-0-448-45731-4 (pbk)   10 9 8 7 6 5 4 3 2 1
ISBN 978-0-448-45741-3 (hc)   10 9 8 7 6 5 4 3 2 1

THE TIME-TRAVELING ADVENTURES OF THE ROBBINS TWINS

THE TREASURE CHEST

AMELIA EARHART: LADY LINDY

-BOOK 8-

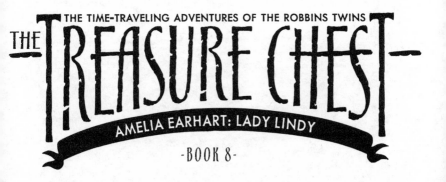

THE TIME-TRAVELING ADVENTURES OF THE ROBBINS TWINS

THE TREASURE CHEST

AMELIA EARHART: LADY LINDY

-BOOK 8-

BY *NEW YORK TIMES* BEST-SELLING AUTHOR
ANN HOOD

Grosset & Dunlap
An Imprint of Penguin Group (USA) LLC

For Annabelle at Eight

CHAPTER 1

THE CRUCIBLE

Maisie had survived a fire at sea. She'd escaped to Shanghai during the Boxer Rebellion, avoided arrows and lava, and managed to get out of a workhouse in London. *Why,* she thought, *I've even survived my parents' divorce and moving to Newport, Rhode Island, and being the new kid in school!* And she had hardly been afraid at all. During all of that. But what Miss Percy was asking her to do terrified her.

"Come on, Maisie," Miss Percy said in her strong, aristocratic Boston accent, the one that Maisie's mother said sounded like she was one of the Kennedys.

She could be JFK's sister, the way she talks, Maisie's mother had said after parent–teacher night. She said it like it wasn't a good thing, even though it seemed to Maisie that being related to President Kennedy would be a very good thing.

"You would be perfect as one of the girls," Miss Percy persisted.

"I don't want to be in the school play," Maisie said.

What she meant was that the idea of getting up on the stage in front of the entire school—all those people who thought she was weird—and saying lines made her shake with fear and dread.

"But it's *The Crucible*!" Miss Percy said as if that mattered.

Of course Maisie knew the play was *The Crucible*. That was all Bitsy Beal talked about these days, how she was going to get the role of Abigail Williams, which was the lead, Maisie assumed, or Bitsy Beal wouldn't want it so badly.

"Arthur Miller!" Miss Percy continued, except she said it like "Ah-tha Mill-ah." "One of the leading American playwrights of the twentieth century!"

"I'm sure he's a very good writer," Maisie said. "I just don't want to be onstage, that's all."

Miss Percy had dirty-blond hair cut in a chin-

"Is Rayne auditioning, too?" Felix asked hopefully.

"Of course!" Hadley said. "Maisie, which part are you going to read for?"

"I . . . um . . ."

"She doesn't want to audition," Felix said.

"I . . . ," Maisie began.

But she couldn't say anything more. She had grown up with a mother who'd had one glorious season in summer-stock theater, playing every lead role in every play. Even though her mother was a lawyer now, Maisie remembered when she still tried to be an actress back in New York. She remembered her mother practicing lines for auditions, acting in showcases where agents went to try to find talent, taking roles in plays in tiny theaters off-off-off Broadway. Maisie used to be awed by her mother's ability to memorize monologues and turn into a different person onstage, a murderer or a very old woman or once even an apple tree. But the thought of doing those things herself? In front of everyone at the Anne Hutchinson Elementary School? No way.

"—or you could be Betty or Ruth," Hadley was saying. "They get to go into strange stupors, which is really cool."

Hadley hung her tongue out one side of her mouth, crossed her eyes, and held her arms out zombie style to demonstrate.

"I don't want to be in the stupid play!" Maisie said much more harshly than she intended.

Embarrassed, she walked away from Felix and Hadley as fast as she could and went into Mrs. Witherspoon's classroom.

"What brings you here three minutes early, Miss Robbins?" Mrs. Witherspoon said, surprised.

"I'm sick of everybody talking about *The Crucible*," Maisie said, slumping into her seat.

Mrs. Witherspoon leveled her stone gaze on Maisie.

"You would be wonderful as Abigail Williams," Mrs. Witherspoon said in her dry voice. "Abigail Williams is smart, wily, and a very good liar."

"Thanks a lot," Maisie muttered under her breath.

"And," Mrs. Witherspoon continued, "she is vindictive when crossed."

"Vindictive?" Maisie asked, mildly curious.

"She likes to get even," Mrs. Witherspoon explained. "For example, if Bitsy Beal were making her life miserable, Abigail would get even."

Mrs. Witherspoon held Maisie's stare until Maisie blinked first.

The second bell rang and everyone spilled into the classroom. But Mrs. Witherspoon did not look away from Maisie's surprised face.

Earlier in the year, they'd had an assembly about peer pressure. The school nurse, Miss Patty, a round redhead with a slight southern twang, had stood on the stage in the auditorium and showed the school a movie on bullying with bad actors pretending to be middle school kids. Then she showed an animated movie in which cartoon hedgehogs got peer-pressured into doing things appropriate for other animals but not for hedgehogs, like swimming and flying.

Most of the kids had laughed or passed notes back and forth or even napped. Miss Patty's pink face got pinker and pinker as she realized no one was really paying attention. Even though she wasn't a real nurse, Miss Patty always wore a nurse's uniform with white stockings and weird white shoes. Her body was round. Her face was round. Even her hair, pale and thin and red, was cut in a way that made it look round, too.

"Come on!" Miss Patty had whined. "Pay attention."

But no one did. Why would middle schoolers pay attention to cartoon hedgehogs trying to swim?

That assembly made Maisie angry. Even though the actors in the first movie were terrible, when a gang of them laughed at the weird girl, Maisie's stomach lurched. Bitsy Beal and her friends had been laughing at Maisie since she'd come to this school, hadn't they? Which meant that Maisie had been bullied, an idea that made her so mad she wanted to stand up and scream.

At least she didn't give in to peer pressure, she thought as she watched one of the hedgehogs jump off the branch of a tree, flap his little hedgehog arms, and fall straight to the ground. Everyone laughed, but Maisie even felt mad at that cartoon hedgehog. *Stand up for yourself!* she'd told him silently.

Now Maisie found herself in the auditorium after school, clutching that pale blue script, with everyone else. She absolutely did not want to be in *The Crucible*. Or any play, for that matter. But here she was, listening to Miss Percy talk about the Salem witch trials and Arthur Miller and the Puritans as if it mattered.

When Miss Percy said: "Many people believe that *The Crucible* is an allegory for Communism," Bitsy Beal smiled and nodded and made sure everyone noticed her.

Miss Percy continued, "Arthur Miller says he wrote the play in response to the McCarthy hearings in the 1950s. You'll learn much more about McCarthyism in middle school. For now, let's just focus on auditions." Maisie leaned back in the creaky chair and sighed. Wasn't she giving in to peer pressure by being here? Had she become nothing more than a dumb animated hedgehog?

"So here's how this works," Miss Percy said, her eyes shining. "I call you up in groups of two or three and have you read some of the lines together. You might be called up here many times or just once. What I'm looking for is how you inhabit the different roles, how you look with the other people up here on the stage."

"You're deciding who will play which part," Bitsy said, overstating the obvious.

"Yes, Bitsy," Miss Percy said. "I'm casting the play. That's why we're all here."

Bitsy looked smug, but Maisie sat up a little bit

taller. Miss Percy had just kind of put Bitsy Beal in her place, hadn't she? And Bitsy didn't even realize it.

Miss Percy began to call kids to the stage. She placed Felix to the right and had Rayne Ziff read with him. Then she made Felix stay there and had Bitsy read with him. Then she had Felix sit down and Jim Duncan read with Bitsy. And on and on for maybe the most boring half hour Maisie could remember.

"Okay, Maisie," Miss Percy finally said. "Come on up here."

Maisie got that throwing-up feeling as she walked to the stage. She paused and took several deep breaths to calm her stomach. Throwing up in front of everyone would be worse than anything.

Jim Duncan was standing there, grinning.

"So Jim, you read John Proctor, and Maisie, you read Abigail," Miss Percy said.

Jim read his lines smoothly, but why wouldn't he? Maisie thought. He'd been standing up here forever practicing.

When Maisie opened her mouth, a strange croaking sound came out. Someone in the audience giggled.

"The town's mumbling witchcraft," Jim said again.

"Oh posh," Maisie said in a voice that did not sound like her own.

Miss Percy walked over to Jim and Maisie with her long, purposeful stride.

"A little louder, Maisie," she offered, except she said "loud-ah."

She put her strong hands on Maisie's shoulders and gave a squeeze.

"You'll do just fine," Miss Percy whispered.

When Miss Percy strode off, Jim Duncan repeated, "The town's mumbling witchcraft."

Maisie took another deep breath.

"Oh posh!" she said, nice and loud.

She could hear her heartbeat ringing in her ears.

The stage directions told her to get closer to John Proctor and to speak winningly and with a wicked air.

Maisie stood as close to Jim Duncan as she dared.

"We were dancing in the woods last night," she recited as winningly and wickedly as she could muster.

The room had gone oddly quiet.

"She took fright is all," Maisie finished.

Jim Duncan smiled, just like the directions told him.

"Ah, you're wicked yet," he said, sending goose bumps up Maisie's arms.

As Jim kept talking, everything except his voice and the words on the page disappeared. It was as if she *was* Abigail Williams and Jim Duncan *was* John Proctor.

"Give me a word, John," Maisie said, moving even closer to him and trying to look feverishly into his eyes like Arthur Miller told her to do. "A soft word," Maisie finished.

Jim Duncan turned from her. "No—no, Abby, I've not come for that."

For a moment, even though there were no more lines for them, Jim and Maisie both stood, feeling the power of what they had said.

Then, just as quickly, the spell was broken.

"Thank you, Maisie," Miss Percy said. "Jim, stay up there. Hadley, read Abigail, please."

For the next hour, Maisie sat in the audience as kids were called up, rearranged, asked to read this part and that part. But Miss Percy never called her back up to the stage.

"Mercy Lewis is a good role," Felix said optimistically as he and Maisie walked to school the next morning.

He thought his sister had read the part of Abigail Williams better than anybody else. But when Miss Percy didn't ask her to read anything else, or with any other boys, he knew that she was going to get a tiny part. Everyone knew.

"Mercy Lewis is the smallest, most insignificant part in the entire play," Maisie said. She knew Felix was trying to make her feel better. But she'd read that whole stupid blue book last night and getting the part of Mercy Lewis would be practically an embarrassment.

"Small," Felix said quickly. "But not insignificant. None of the girls in Abigail's group are insignificant."

"Oh please," Maisie muttered.

"Actually," Felix said, changing course, "since you don't really want to be in the play and Miss Percy knows that, she's probably doing you a favor by casting you in a minor role. You won't have a lot to do or say and—"

"Maybe I do want to be in the dumb play!" Maisie blurted. "Maybe I just have stage fright!"

To her surprise, she started to cry. How could she describe to Felix or to anybody how she felt up there reading those lines yesterday? Like she'd become a different person. Once her throat stopped being so dry and her heart stopped pounding, Maisie had felt transported. No. Transformed. By the time she stepped off the stage, she wanted nothing more to be cast in *The Crucible*. And even worse, she wanted to be Abigail Williams.

Felix was patting her shoulder and cooing, "You read really well, Maisie. Honest you did."

"Then why am I going to be Mercy Lewis?" Maisie sobbed. She shrugged away from Felix's hands and made her own lonely way to school. Behind her, Maisie heard Jim Duncan calling for her to wait up, but she just kept walking.

But when Maisie got to school, she didn't go inside. Instead, she leaned against the brick building, trying to collect herself. Was it worse, she wondered, to have the smallest, most insignificant part in the play? Or to not be in the play at all and have to endure two months of Felix and everybody else going to rehearsals and cast parties and talking about nothing but the stupid *Crucible*? Maisie finally had a friend in Hadley Ziff, and maybe even Rayne but they, too, would be swept up in the play, leaving Maisie once again on the outside, alone.

No, Maisie decided, she had to do it. She had to put on a dumb bonnet and stand in the background as Mercy Lewis while Bitsy Beal stole the show. Her mother used to say, "There are no small parts, just small actors," whenever she didn't get a big role, which was almost always. And Maisie's father would add, "There are no small parts, just small paychecks," and then they would both laugh ruefully because usually her mother got no paycheck at all for her acting.

From the corner of her eye, Maisie saw Felix and Jim Duncan arrive and go inside. She sighed. *Okay, Mercy Lewis,* Maisie thought, *go on in.*

The first thing Maisie saw when she stepped into the school's lobby was a crowd gathered around the cast list Miss Percy had posted.

"I'm going to class," Maisie muttered.

But before she could walk away, Bitsy Beal angrily barreled right into her.

"Excuse me," Maisie said sarcastically.

Bitsy's eyes were red and her cheeks were wet

with tears. But her face looked mad enough to knock Maisie over.

"You!" Bitsy said. "You . . . nothing! You no-talent, no-friend, scene-stealer!"

"What?" Maisie said, bewildered.

Bitsy stormed off, and slowly Maisie became aware that every single person was staring at her.

"What?" she said again.

From the crowd, Jim Duncan emerged with a big, silly grin on his face.

"John Proctor," he said, holding his hand out to Maisie. "Pleased to meet you, Abigail Williams."

"What?" Maisie said for a third time.

"You got the part!" Felix shrieked. "You're Abigail!"

The next thing she knew, Felix and Jim Duncan and the Ziff twins and almost everybody else were hugging Maisie.

They were congratulating her and gushing about her audition, their faces all happy and excited.

But all Maisie could do was think: *I got the part, I got the part, I got the part* while she tried not to throw up.

CHAPTER 2

AMY PICKWORTH

Once Great-Uncle Thorne discovered that the Ziff twins were descendants of Amy Pickworth, he started to change his mind about some things. First, he changed his mind about Maisie and Felix and their mother moving back upstairs to the servants' quarters. *Pickworths belong in Elm Medona!* he announced, and they all unpacked everything they had just packed up and settled back into their old rooms. Then he changed his mind about The Treasure Chest. He unsealed it and kept it unsealed. *Pickworths have a gift, a responsibility, a calling!* he decided. Then he changed his mind about the Ziff twins. *Pickworths need to stick together!*

Added to his excitement about finding new Pickworths was the excitement about his upcoming wedding to Penelope Merriweather. And, of course, Maisie and Felix's father's wedding to Agatha the Great. It was hard not to feel excited, too, Felix thought. But Maisie was not excited. She was mad.

Maisie was going to be a junior bridesmaid, not once but twice. This would be fine, maybe even thrilling, except for the fact that Felix was going to be a best man. Twice. And on the importance scale for weddings, best man was much higher than junior bridesmaid.

"Can't I be a real bridesmaid?" Maisie asked her father.

"I don't really know how this all works," he admitted. "But Agatha said junior bridesmaid, which I think just refers to your age. Maybe you can't be a full-blown bridesmaid until you're old enough to vote?"

"That," Maisie said, "is ridiculous."

"Can't I be a real bridesmaid?" Maisie asked Great-Uncle Thorne that night at supper.

"No," he answered, his mouth full of *moules*, which were actually mussels. But he insisted on calling them by their French name.

"Maybe you'll think about it?" Maisie said.

She took a mussel out of its shell with the special little fork that was used for just this purpose, and stared at it. Yellow and slimy with some blue around the edges. She put it back in its shiny black shell and waited.

"There's nothing to think about," Great-Uncle Thorne said. "Read your Emily Post."

"My what?" Maisie asked.

Across the table, Felix plopped mussels into his mouth. How could someone who did not like eggs or mayonnaise or anything normal eat these disgusting blobs? Maisie looked away.

"Etiquette, my dear girl," Great-Uncle Thorne said, tossing his empty shell into the sterling silver bowl with the interlocking *P*s engraved in it. "Eleven-year-olds—"

"I'm twelve," Maisie corrected him.

"*Children*," he said, dipping a fresh mussel into the broth beneath the pile of *moules*, "are junior bridesmaids."

"But then how can Felix be your best man?" Maisie persisted.

Great-Uncle Thorne sighed dramatically.

"Number one," he said, holding up his liver-spotted hand and raising one finger, "all of my friends are dead. Number two, I rather like the lad. He'll be a fine best man."

"*Merci,*" Felix said, chewing a *moule*.

"What?" Maisie said. "You speak French now?"

"Geez," Felix said, "everyone can say *thank you* in French."

Great-Uncle Thorne gently placed his special mussel-plucking fork onto the edge of his bowl.

"You really are an unpleasant young woman," he said. "Penelope has gone to great lengths to get you the most lovely moiré silk for your junior bridesmaid dress, and all you can do is complain. Complain and demand and scowl."

With that, he resumed eating.

Maisie watched him chew. He chewed like an old man, she decided, which of course he was.

"It's rude to stare at someone who is eating," Great-Uncle Thorne said without even looking at her.

"I wish I could just fly away from here," Maisie announced, even though she didn't *really* wish that because then she wouldn't get to be the lead in *The Crucible.*

"If you do," Great-Uncle Thorne said, "please wait until after the wedding."

Her mother was no help at all. Even though she had been the instigator of the divorce, now that Maisie's father was getting married, she acted like he had no right to do that.

"Um," Maisie had reminded her mother, "didn't *you* want the dumb divorce in the first place?"

"It's one thing to want a divorce and to get a divorce and to actually be happier divorced, and it's another thing to realize that your husband is going to marry another woman," her mother had said, which made no sense at all to Maisie.

"*Ex*-husband," Maisie had said.

"I know," her mother had agreed with a sigh. "I guess it's just the reality of the situation."

Maisie had chalked this up to one of those weird adult things she didn't understand.

Earlier, Maisie had asked her mother's opinion of what a junior bridesmaid's duties were. Did she think they were different than a bridesmaid's duties? Did junior bridesmaids get to walk down the aisle with grown-up men? Or was there some kind of junior-male thing as well? She imagined someone younger, shorter, in every way more junior than herself. Would she have to hold his arm? Sit with him? Dance with him?

"I really don't want to discuss your father's wedding, if that's okay with you, Maisie," her mother had said primly.

"Well, then can we discuss this in terms of Great-Uncle Thorne's wedding, where I am also a junior bridesmaid?" Maisie demanded.

"I have a brief to write," her mother had said, picking up her briefcase and heading upstairs, which wasn't an answer; it was an excuse.

As if he'd read her mind, Great-Uncle Thorne said, "Where is your mother? Out with that Fishbaum fellow?"

"She's working," Felix said.

"All of a sudden the reality of her divorcing Dad has hit her, and she does not want to talk about it," Maisie said.

Great-Uncle Thorne looked perplexed.

"I think all the wedding planning is wearing on her," Felix added.

"Ah," Great-Uncle Thorne said, nodding. "Ditto Penelope."

He ate more mussels.

"I've done some research," he said after he rang the bell for the table to be cleared.

"On?" Maisie asked.

"Your friends. Your . . . what's their surname? Zinger?"

"Ziff," Felix said.

"Yes, them. The Ziff twins. Amy Pickworth's descendants."

He paused.

Maisie and Felix waited.

"As you know, we always assumed that Amy Pickworth met her demise in the Congo."

They nodded.

"She and Phinneas had gone there to acquire artifacts for The Treasure Chest," Great-Uncle Thorne continued. "According to my father, they spent the night in a hut with some natives, and in the morning she had vanished. He claims that he searched for her along the river and in the jungle, but not even a trace turned up. Except . . ."

He paused again and began fumbling in his pocket.

"Except?" Maisie asked eagerly.

"Except for this," Great-Uncle Thorne said, and finally removed from his pocket a piece of heavy vellum paper with two words written on it in faded black ink:

gone black A O

"'Gone black'," Felix read out loud. "'A O'."

"What does that mean?" Maisie asked.

"We assumed of course that it meant they killed her. 'Gone black' standing in for imminent death. 'A O' her initials. Amy Olivia."

"How sad," Felix said softly.

Maisie shook her head. "It doesn't make sense," she said, thinking out loud. "She had time to write a farewell note? These natives are . . . I don't know . . . throwing spears at her or getting ready to eat her or shrink her head and she has time to write that note in that fancy handwriting?"

Great-Uncle Thorne looked at her, impressed. "Bravo. You have to be right. Amy Pickworth wrote that note with care, I'd say. Under duress, even excellent penmanship would waver."

Felix picked up the note and began to read it silently, his lips moving as he did.

"But what else could it mean?" Maisie wondered.

"I think your brother there is about to tell us," Great-Uncle Thorne said, a satisfied smile spreading across his face.

"It's an anagram, isn't it?" Felix said.

"Spoken like a true Pickworth!" Great-Uncle Thorne said with obvious pride.

Maisie took the note from her brother and stared at the letters there. Almost immediately, they seemed to reshape themselves, revealing their meaning to her.

"'Go back alone'," Maisie read.

She looked at Great-Uncle Thorne and said the words again: "'Go back alone'."

"Amy Pickworth stayed in that jungle intentionally," Great-Uncle Thorne said. His great white brows furrowed. "The question I have is *why?*"

As much as Maisie wanted more duties as a junior bridesmaid, Felix wanted fewer duties as a best man. Just yesterday, Great-Uncle Thorne had handed him a dusty book that looked like no one had opened in about a million years. When Great-Uncle Thorne cracked the spine, the first pages crumbled. Undeterred, he'd carefully turned the brittle pages until he found what he was looking for.

"Here," he told Felix, sliding the book across the table.

There, under the heading, DUTIES OF A BEST MAN, a list stretched. There were duties for planning the wedding and duties during the rehearsal and duties the night before the wedding and before the ceremony and during the ceremony and even at the reception.

"I have to throw you a bachelor party?" Felix said.

Great-Uncle Thorne grinned and nodded.

"I'm only twelve," Felix reminded him.

"Irrelevant!" Great-Uncle Thorne said dismissively.

Felix scanned the never-ending list of duties.

"Arrange accommodations for out-of-town groomsmen?" Felix read.

"The Viking Hotel is always nice," Great-Uncle Thorne offered.

When Felix showed Maisie the list the next night after dinner, she was dismissive, too.

"There won't be any groomsmen," she told Felix. "He doesn't have any friends or relatives except you."

"Dad does," Felix said.

"Junior bridesmaids just walk down the aisle," Maisie said. "Probably in an ugly dress."

"I have to organize the wedding toasts," Felix said. "The bride's father gives the first one—"

"Penelope Merriweather's father died on the *Titanic*," Maisie reminded him. "And Gramps died before we were even born."

"Then I give the second toast," Felix continued as if she hadn't spoken. "Then who should come next?"

Maisie brightened. "I'll give the toast after you."

"Really?" Felix said, checking at least that one duty off his list.

"I'd better get started," Maisie said, her mind already swirling with quotes she could use. Her teacher, Mrs. Witherspoon, had taught them that every good speech starts with a quote.

She began to jot down the ones she knew offhand. *Ask not what your country can do for you, ask what you can do for your country . . . Four score and seven years ago . . . Friends, Romans, countrymen, lend me your ears . . .*

"What?" Felix asked her.

Maisie glanced up at her brother.

"What do you mean 'what'?" she asked him.

"Your eyebrows are all crinkled like something's wrong," he said.

Maisie sighed. "I don't know the first thing about love," she said. "I'm going to have get a book of love poems. Who writes love poems?"

"Um," Felix said.

"Exactly."

The next morning, their mother did not emerge from her bedroom. Aiofe reported that she was working at home.

"'Do not disturb,'" Aiofe announced as she refilled Maisie's hot cocoa. "That's what she said."

"I don't think Mom has worked at home since we moved here—" Felix began.

"Ever," Maisie interrupted.

"Should we call the doctor?" Felix asked, worried.

Just then Great-Uncle Thorne walked in to the dining room.

"She'll be fine once the hubbub dies down," he said. "Why, Penelope won't even take a stroll with me this morning." He shook his head. "A real shame, too, because the Pickworth peonies have all bloomed." Great-Uncle Thorne gave a small, satisfied smile. "Just in time for the wedding, too."

"Won't Penelope want the Merriweather roses for the wedding?" Maisie asked.

"Don't be ridiculous," Great-Uncle Thorne said. "Have you *seen* our peonies this year? They are truly magnificent."

He took his seat at the head of the table, flicked a linen napkin open and tucked it into his collar.

"Mmmm," he said, reaching for the silver serving tray. "Shirred eggs."

"I don't understand why Mom is so mad about Dad getting married," Felix wondered out loud. "She's got Bruce Fishbaum."

"It's complicated," Great-Uncle Thorne said. "Every one of Phinneas Pickworth's ex-wives got angry when he married a new woman."

"How many times did he get married?" Maisie asked him.

Great-Uncle Thorne waved his bony hand dismissively. "It doesn't matter. He always loved our mother, Ariane, above all others."

His eyes stayed on Aiofe, following her as she made sure everyone had what they needed before she left to get fresh coffee.

Once she was gone, Great-Uncle Thorne leaned forward and said in a stage whisper, "Get those Ziff twins over here. I'm sending you all on a mission."

Felix groaned. How could he possibly do even one more thing?

But Maisie was intrigued. "What kind of mission?" she asked.

Great-Uncle Thorne cocked his head, listening to be sure Aiofe wasn't approaching before he spoke.

"Upstairs," he said, "in The Treasure Chest, there's something that will bring you to the Congo—"

"And Amy Pickworth!" Maisie said, excited.

Great-Uncle Thorne nodded solemnly. "And Amy Pickworth. I want you to find it and go there immediately."

"What's the object?" Felix asked.

Aiofe's footsteps neared.

"I don't know for certain," Great-Uncle Thorne admitted. "I only know they went to find Dr. Livingstone."

Maisie and Felix glanced at each other and shrugged.

"My sister was right," Great-Uncle Thorne said. "You two know nothing about anything at all."

Aiofe walked in with more coffee and cocoa.

"After school," Great-Uncle Thorne said, leveling his gaze on Maisie and then Felix. "Meet me in the Library. And bring those Ziff twins."

CHAPTER 3

THE MISSION

Maisie's teacher, Mrs. Witherspoon, clapped her hands for attention.

"People!" she said. Then louder: "People!"

Maisie caught Hadley's eye and the two of them smirked.

"Today we are starting a new unit," Mrs. Witherspoon announced when the noise died down.

Still looking at Maisie, Hadley crossed her eyes and stuck out her tongue.

"Miss Ziff?" Mrs. Witherspoon said. "Is there a problem?"

"Oh no," Hadley said sweetly. "I can't wait to hear about it."

Mrs. Witherspoon studied Hadley's face for a moment before she continued.

"The new unit is on aviation," she said, pulling the large world map down over the blackboard.

Inwardly, Maisie groaned. *Aviation?* she thought. *Seriously?*

". . . Charles Lindbergh . . . ," Mrs. Witherspoon was saying.

Surely there would be a report of some kind, Maisie thought. Mrs. Witherspoon loved reports and oral presentations.

". . . the Space Age . . . ," Mrs. Witherspoon was saying. "Your topic for your report can span the centuries!"

A smile crept over Maisie's face. The Aviatrix Room! Right in Elm Medona. Her mother's bedroom was the Aviatrix Room. It had real airplane wings suspended from the ceiling and an entire cabinet of early aviation mementos. *My room is sepia,* her mother had complained when they'd first moved into the mansion from the servant's quarters. Maisie hadn't known what "sepia" was until her mother threw open the door to the Aviatrix Room and said: *Look! Sepia walls and draperies and . . . everything!*

Sepia was brown. The brown of old photographs and maps. And the Aviatrix Room was indeed sepia. Except the ceiling, which was the most beautiful blue Maisie had ever seen. The way those airplane wings were suspended from that ceiling, it actually looked as if a plane was disappearing into the sky.

"Where do you go, Miss Robbins?" Mrs. Witherspoon asked wearily.

Maisie glanced around the room. Everyone seemed to be staring at her, waiting.

"Uh," she said.

"Miss Perkins is interested in doing a report on Neil Armstrong. Mr. Cooper wants to study Juan Tripp," Mrs. Witherspoon said.

She leveled her gaze on Maisie. "I don't suppose *you* have any ideas, Miss Robbins?"

Maisie grinned. "Either Brave Bessie Colman, Pancho Barnes, or Amy Johnson," she said, naming the women pilots whose mementos were in her mother's bedroom. Mrs. Witherspoon looked bewildered.

"They're aviatrixes," Maisie said smugly. "Female—"

"I know what an aviatrix is, Miss Robbins," Mrs.

Witherspoon said. "I'm just surprised that you know of so many."

"Oh," Maisie said, "you'd be surprised at the things I know."

As soon as Maisie's class entered the library, Felix grabbed his sister's arm and pulled her into the stacks. His class was also doing a unit on aviation, and Miss Landers had brought them to the library to start researching their subjects, too. But Felix had looked up Dr. Livingstone instead.

"Malaria," he whispered to Maisie. "Cannibals."

Maisie shook her head. "Our unit's on aviation," she explained.

"Not the unit!" Felix said. "The Congo!"

When Maisie still looked confused, Felix said, "Dr. Livingstone. He went to Africa in 1871 to find the source of the Nile and he died there, just like every other explorer."

"You mean Great-Uncle Thorne's Dr. Livingstone?"

Exasperated, he said, "Yes, yes. That Dr. Livingstone. And I am not going to the Congo. No way."

Images of Africa filled Maisie's mind. She'd seen enough documentaries on the Nature Channel to have vivid images of herds of charging elephants and migrating wildebeests and prowling lions.

"I think it sounds kind of dreamy," she said.

"This other guy? Stanley? He went to find Dr. Livingstone and got cerebral malaria, which is a million times worse than plain old malaria. Then he got smallpox!"

"I don't think you can get smallpox anymore," Maisie said, thinking of giraffes with their long eyelashes and long necks.

"Are you even listening to me?"

"I think it would be extremely cool to go to Africa," she said firmly.

"Maybe now. On a safari or something. But not in 1871 when warring tribes are massacring one another, and crocodiles are eating people and—"

"Felix," Maisie said, putting her hand on her brother's shoulder, "you worry too much."

With that, she turned and left the stacks.

Felix watched in disbelief as she walked away. He was certain of one thing: Great-Uncle Thorne would not be able to convince him to go to the Congo.

The shard had become a bit of a problem for Maisie, who had somehow become the person in charge of it. Sure, when it was cooler and she'd worn her polar fleece vest over almost anything, it had been easy to keep the shard in her pocket. But now that it was warmer, she almost never wore the vest, and she frequently found herself pocket-less.

That afternoon, before the Ziff twins arrived, she'd stared at the thing for some time, trying to figure out what to do with it so that it was safe and conveniently located should time traveling be in her future, which it was, thanks to Great-Uncle Thorne.

Maisie picked up the delicate white porcelain with the broken pattern of blue flowers on it and studied it closely.

What was that thing at the top?

She held the shard up to her eyes, closing one to focus better.

There, at the top, was the tiniest hole.

Maisie smiled, satisfied.

Tucking the shard into her fist, she went downstairs, all the way to the Kitchen in the basement. It smelled disgusting.

"What are you cooking?" Maisie asked, wrinkling her nose.

"Your great-uncle Thorne has requested a *pot-au-feu* for dinner tonight," Cook said without bothering to look at Maisie.

"Pot-oh-what?"

Cook clucked her tongue and shook her head.

Maisie peered over her shoulder. Chunks of meat bounced around in a pot of boiling water, leaving a disgusting tan froth on their wake.

"Ugh!" Maisie said. "Are you boiling meat?"

"A *pot-au-feu* requires salting the short ribs a day in advance," Cook said. "Then blanching them before braising. *This*," she added, disgusted by Maisie's ignorance, "is blanching, not boiling."

"Whatever," Maisie said, eyeballing the chopping board lined with all sorts of disgusting root vegetables, like turnips and . . .

"What are these?" Maisie asked, poking at the hard purple-and-beige vegetable.

Cook sighed. "Rutabagas," she answered wearily. "Did you need something? Or have you come downstairs to critique my delicious preparation of a *pot-au-feu*?"

"Thread," Maisie said. "I need some thread."

Cook pointed toward a distant drawer where Maisie found spools of fine thread in every color imaginable. Her hand hesitated over first red, then purple, before settling on black. She pocketed the spool of black thread and headed out.

"Thanks," she called over her shoulder.

"You *will* be returning that," Cook said unpleasantly.

Back in her room, Maisie licked the end of the thread and twisted it so that it was narrow enough to fit through the tiny hole in the shard.

"Perfect," she said as she held up her new necklace.

Maisie tied the thread in a triple knot at the back of her neck. The shard hung cool between her collarbones. Satisfied, she ran downstairs to greet the Ziff twins.

"You make a plan," Great-Uncle Thorne told Maisie and Felix and Hadley and Rayne. "And then you execute it."

They were all standing at the wall, right by where you pressed to make it open and reveal the stairs that led to The Treasure Chest.

He snickered at Maisie and Felix.

"That's what you two never figured out," he said, his voice full of disdain. "You went in there willy-nilly, picking objects up at random and stumbling through time."

Insulted, Maisie put her hands on her hips and glared at Great-Uncle Thorne. "Well, nobody told us anything," she said. "We had no idea—"

"I told you how to utilize *lame demon*, didn't I? But still you just grabbed at anything—"

"It was a crown," Felix said. "Not just anything."

"—and you went where?" Great-Uncle Thorne continued as if Felix hadn't spoken. "And for what purpose?"

"Why did you ask us to come here?" Hadley said.

Rayne, who had looked bored until now, came to life.

"Are you sending us on a mission?" she asked, her blue eyes shining.

"You see," Great-Uncle said, looking dreamily at some distant point, "my sister and I would plan. We'd come back from a visit to the Metropolitan Museum of Art where we'd fallen in love with a painting and we'd say, 'Van Gogh. Let's find Van Gogh.' That was the fun of it, you see? To enter The Treasure Chest and, almost like a scavenger hunt or a puzzle, have to find just the right object to reach that person. That's the way Phinneas wanted it. He loved games and puzzles, you know," Great-Uncle Thorne added.

"So we've heard," Maisie muttered.

"It was exciting," Great-Uncle Thorne said sadly. "It was a challenge."

Rayne had gone back to chipping the purple nail polish off her fingernails. But Hadley seemed thoughtful.

"You want us to go—" she began.

"To the Congo!" Felix blurted. "Where there's malaria and cannibals and dangerous natives!"

Once more, Rayne grew excited. "Now that's an adventure. What do we need to do?"

"He thinks Amy Pickworth is there," Maisie said.

"I *know* she's there," Great-Uncle Thorne said, pointing a finger at Maisie.

"You want us to find her?" Rayne asked at the very same time that Hadley said, "And do what with her?"

Great-Uncle Thorne leveled his gaze on each of them, one at a time. A chill ran up Felix's spine when that gaze lingered on him.

"Bring her home," Great-Uncle Thorne said matter-of-factly.

"But even if we find her, which seems pretty much impossible, she can't come back with us," Felix said nervously. "You need your twin with you."

Great-Uncle Thorne nodded slowly.

Felix held up his hands. "Well then," he said.

"All I know for certain," Great-Uncle Thorne said thoughtfully, "is that you need your twin to get *there*."

Again, he stared off at some distant place.

Then he looked at them again and his voice grew firm.

"I came back without my twin, didn't I?" he asked.

Maisie knew that it was a rhetorical question, but she still said, "That's right, you did."

"Came back from where?" Hadley asked, trying to keep up.

"New York," Felix explained. "We all went there, Maisie and me and Great-Uncle Thorne and—"

"And my bullheaded sister," Great-Uncle

Thorne interrupted. "For decades she carried a torch for that nincompoop Harry Houdini—"

"Your sister had a crush on Harry Houdini?" Rayne asked, interested again.

Great-Uncle Thorne banged his walking stick on the floor.

"Irrelevant!" he proclaimed. "All that you need to know is that Amy Pickworth can come back without her twin, just like I returned without that obdurate sister of mine."

"Obdurate?" Rayne said, losing interest again.

"Oh! Look it up!" Great-Uncle Thorne said dismissively. "We have more to do here than improve your vocabulary."

While Great-Uncle Thorne shouted, Rayne stepped forward, her palm facing outward as if she was ready at any moment to press that spot on the wall and go up those stairs.

"I'm coming upstairs with you," Great-Uncle Thorne said quickly. "We'll survey the objects and find the one that will get you to the Congo."

"But surely that object is gone," Felix said. "Phinneas and Amy took it with them to get there in the first place."

Great-Uncle Thorne shook his head. "They hadn't given the object to Dr. Livingstone when Amy disappeared," he said.

"You're wrong!" Felix said, his head swimming with too much information.

"I'm certain of this."

Maisie's face had that deep-in-thought look she got when she was thinking hard.

"Impossible," she finally said. "Phinneas could not get back if they hadn't given the object and received a lesson."

Great-Uncle Thorne's face twisted with anger.

"You are an idiot!" he said. "That's why you have *lame demon*!"

"I thought it was—"

Great-Uncle Thorne pressed the wall, hard. As soon as it opened to reveal the staircase, he marched forward to the stairs, his ebony walking stick tap-tapping as he moved.

At the foot of the stairs he paused to face them.

"We will find the object that Phinneas brought back from that fateful trip to the Congo. You will choose a secondary object to bring along. And if and when things become . . . complicated . . . you will say *lame demon* three times with your hand on that secondary object and continue your travels elsewhere."

"Complicated?" Felix asked. "You mean cannibals catching us or—"

"I'm not sure I want to do this," Hadley said.

"Exactly!" Felix agreed.

"I'm in," Maisie said quietly.

"Maisie," Felix pleaded, "let's discuss this calmly and rationally."

"I'm in," she said again, louder this time.

"Maisie," Felix said, and even though he put on the look that usually softened her, this time she shook her head.

"I'm in, too," Rayne said.

Felix didn't like how her fingernails all had half-peeled-off purple nail polish. He didn't like how she wasn't looking at him.

"What?" Rayne asked him. "Don't look at me so weird."

Felix turned away, confused. All of a sudden, he missed Lily Goldberg. Lily Goldberg had not sent him one email or letter or anything since she'd moved away. At first, he'd missed her like crazy.

Then she'd kind of faded into a happy blur. But standing here right now, seeing Rayne's messy fingernails and listening to Great-Uncle Thorne's big plans, the threat of the Congo getting closer every second, Felix wanted nothing more than to talk to Lily.

The others were following Great-Uncle Thorne up the stairs to The Treasure Chest and, for a crazy moment, Felix thought he might just walk away. They couldn't do this without him, could they?

Great-Uncle Thorne paused on the stairs and swiveled his head so that he faced Felix below.

"What are you waiting for?" he bellowed.

Maybe because Felix always did what he was supposed to do, or maybe because everyone else was standing there waiting for him, he scurried to meet them.

Great-Uncle Thorne unclasped the maroon velvet rope and swept his arm to indicate they should all enter The Treasure Chest.

Once everyone had stepped across the threshold, Great-Uncle Thorne strode into the room and began to scan the cupboards and shelves.

An object caught Felix's eye almost immediately.

All of a sudden, he forgot about the Congo and Amy Pickworth. Instead, he remembered his aviation report.

At the end of the day, Miss Landers had made them write down the aviator they wanted to research and Felix chose Charles Lindbergh.

"Ah!" Miss Landers had said, flashing her dazzling smile at him. "Lucky Lindy!"

"Lucky Lindy?" Felix had said.

"That was his nickname," Miss Landers explained.

Jim Duncan signed up for Baron von Richthofen, the World War I flying ace also known as the Red Baron. And Libby announced she would do her project on Chuck Yeager, the first man to break the sound barrier. Even Felix, who had trouble getting excited about the aviation unit because he was so worried about Great-Uncle Thorne's mission, started to relax. *Lucky Lindy*, he thought, liking the way that sounded.

Now, right on the desk in front of him, surrounded by a seashell and a magnifying glass, was a compass. Not a regular compass, but the kind that fit into a dashboard of instruments on a plane.

Maybe it belonged to Lucky Lindy, Felix thought. Hadn't Great-Uncle Thorne said to be more deliberate about the objects they chose? When Felix reached for it, a liver-spotted hand grabbed his wrist, hard.

"No one is touching anything until we find what we are looking for!" Great-Uncle Thorne boomed.

"Um," Maisie said, "what *are* we looking for?"

"How would I know?" Great-Uncle Thorne said dismissively. "When my sister and I wanted to visit King Tutankhamen, we came in here and we searched for an Egyptian object. Therefore—"

"Um," Maisie said, "but how did you manage to get to this King Toot . . . Toot and . . ."

Great-Uncle Thorne slapped his forehead.

"Have you never heard of King Tut, you imbecile?"

"Of course," Maisie said haughtily. "I just never knew his full name."

"I think what Maisie was trying to say," Hadley offered, "is how did you know that an Egyptian amulet or *kartoush* or whatever would get you to King . . . Tut . . . and not to, say, Cleopatra?"

Great-Uncle Thorne blinked. Then blinked again.

"I suppose we made a mistake or two," he admitted. He chuckled softly. "Why, there was the time we ended up on the *Mayflower* instead of the *Santa Maria*. Now that was interesting."

He looked at their blank faces and *tsked*.

"The *Mayflower* brought the Pilgrims to Massachusetts," he said, his voice thick with contempt. "The *Santa Maria* was one of Columbus's ships, along with the *Niña* and the *Pinta*."

"Got it," Rayne said, and she began to walk around the room, studying the objects that crowded every surface.

Maisie went to the other end of The Treasure Chest, scrutinizing an object carefully before deciding it wasn't the right one.

"I think," she said slowly, "that we aren't looking for something African. We're looking for something Dr. Livingstone needed to survive there."

"Like malaria pills?" Felix asked, only half jokingly.

Hadley held up a map, brown with age and crisscrossed with faded blue lines.

"He might have needed this," she said.

Immediately, Great-Uncle Thorne took it from

her. He held it close to his eyes to better examine it.

"The confounded continent has changed so much over time," he said, more to himself than to the children.

Everyone gathered around him, craning their necks to try to get a view of the map.

Everyone except Felix. He stayed put, and as soon as he was certain no one had noticed him, he tucked the compass into the pocket of his hoodie.

"Borders and names back then . . ." He shook his head. "It's hard to make out some of the writing. . . ."

"Wait!" Maisie said, pointing to a particularly long line. "Right there. It says *Nile River*."

"This might be the very thing . . . ," Great-Uncle Thorne said.

With the compass safely in his pocket, Felix joined the others.

"I say we give it a try," Hadley decided.

Great-Uncle Thorne studied the map, then studied the children's faces, then studied the map again.

Finally, with a nod, he looked back up.

Maisie reached for the map, but Great-Uncle Thorne stopped her.

"Remember, I told you to be more thoughtful when you do this," he said firmly. "You know that you are looking for Dr. Livingstone. You know the Congo is a dangerous place."

Felix swallowed hard.

"You know that if you say *lame demon*, you will get out of any predicament."

Great-Uncle Thorne paused.

"You know you may only use that three times."

He held up three fingers and waved them in front of the children.

They all nodded.

"And by all means," Great-Uncle Thorne said in his big voice, "stay together!"

A chill swept over Felix and he shivered. Maisie took his hand and squeezed it.

When Great-Uncle Thorne held the map out to them, a look of nostalgia crossed over his face.

"How I wish I could go with you," he said with a sigh.

Maisie took the map. First Hadley, then Rayne, then Felix put their hands on it, too.

They lifted up, up, up.

The smells of Christmas trees and hot chocolate

and flowers in bloom filled the air.

A breeze blew across them.

Great-Uncle Thorne's upturned face grew smaller and smaller until he vanished altogether and they tumbled through time.

CHAPTER 4

SILVERBACK!

When Maisie looked up, all she saw was green. From somewhere way above her came a tiny pinprick of light. But otherwise, just green. She was looking up because she seemed to be tangled in something that prevented her from looking anywhere else. She wiggled and writhed, trying to free herself, but it seemed the more she moved, the more tangled she became.

Maisie squinted.

The green, she realized, was all leaves. A canopy of thick green leaves hung over her. Over everything, really. In fact, she realized as she struggled to free herself, she seemed to be caught up in foliage of some kind.

Maisie wiggled and writhed some more.

Not just leaves. Vines. She was caught up in vines so strong that she couldn't bend or break them.

"Felix?" she called.

From the distance, she heard a grunt. *Is Felix trapped, too?* Maisie wondered.

"I'm stuck!" she yelled. "In vines and stuff!"

Another grunt.

Maisie tried to stay perfectly still and think. She knew that Felix could be an extraordinary hypochondriac, always thinking he was hurt worse than he was or worrying over getting a terrible deadly disease. But it was possible, she thought, glancing around as best she could, that he had gotten hurt. Vines and foliage, after all, belonged in a jungle. Which was exactly where they had wanted to land—a jungle along the Congo River. Maisie swallowed hard. She had been excited to come to Africa and find Amy Pickworth and Dr. Livingstone. But now that she was here, alone, tangled up in vines, with her brother maybe seriously hurt, she didn't like the idea so much.

Plus, it was hot. A kind of hot she'd never felt before, almost as if the air was an electric blanket, laying on top of everything and generating heat. She started to sweat, and almost immediately she heard buzzing. And then flies circled her. And then they started to land on her and . . .

And? And what? Maisie tried to figure out, wriggling even more to make the flies fly away.

But they didn't budge. In fact, it felt like they were biting her. No, not biting. Licking.

Gross! Maisie thought.

The flies were licking her sweat.

"Yuck!" Maisie shouted, trying to swat at them.

Birds cawed.

The ground beneath her trembled slightly.

"Felix?" Maisie said, softly at first, then louder: "Felix!"

Nothing but that grunting.

The flies nibbled her sweaty neck.

Maisie squeezed her eyes shut and concentrated on just her right arm. If she could get her right arm free, then she might be able to get all of herself free.

She felt like she spent an hour or more trying without any luck to release her arm from the vine's clutches. The flies kept eating her sweat, and the heat felt hotter and every now and then she heard the sound of an animal she did not recognize. Maisie tried not to think about lions or snakes or hippos. She tried not to think about how Mr. Landon, her science teacher last year, had told them that the hippopotamus was one of the most dangerous animals in Africa. *They'll charge you,* Mr. Landon had said. *And you won't be able to outrun them.* Then it had seemed funny, sitting safely in P.S. 3 surrounded by other kids and the smell of books and paint and ink. The image of a hippo running fast had made Maisie laugh. But now, as the earth trembled again and an animal's calls echoed through the air, it didn't seem funny at all.

Frustrated, Maisie stopped being so careful and methodical and just tried to yank her arms free. The vines cut into her and held on tight.

Now she felt an unmistakable trickle of blood on both arms and what sounded like the footsteps of someone running. Or maybe slipping?

Then came a series of yelps and groans before Felix tumbled right past her, slipping and sliding down what Maisie saw was a steep embankment.

"Ugh!" she heard Felix say.

She could turn her head just enough to see him

climbing slowly up toward her, using vines and branches and whatever else he could grab on to so that he wouldn't go falling back downward again.

"I . . . have . . . looked . . . every . . . where," he panted as he finally reached her side.

His face was smudged with dirt and his glasses hung crookedly on his face.

"Just get me out of here," Maisie said. "Please."

Felix took a couple of deep breaths, then straightened his glasses and studied Maisie's predicament. He remembered how a few years back, their mother had gone through a knitting phase, bringing home skeins of yarns and needles and patterns. She would sit after dinner, frowning at the sweater or scarf she was trying to make, all of it turning out ugly and lumpy or full of holes. She always got her yarn tangled, and he and Maisie would help her straighten it out, pulling it through loops and back again, trying to follow its knotty, complicated path.

This is just like that, he told himself. *Pretend you're untangling Mom's yarn.*

Carefully, he lifted a vine and began to send it backward, away from Maisie. Then he did another. The work was slow and frustrating. Just when he thought he'd released one, he saw that it was looped through yet another.

Maisie moaned. "Can't you go faster?"

"I'm trying," he said.

"It is so hot," Maisie complained.

Felix nodded.

Sweat dripped off his forehead and onto his glasses. Flies kept landing on his face and hands. He didn't know when he'd last felt this miserable.

"Are these flies biting me?" he said, knocking them off his nose.

"I think they're eating our sweat," Maisie said, disgusted.

"Do you think they're tsetse flies?" Felix asked, pausing in his work to stare at his sister.

"Maybe?" she said.

"Tsetse flies give you sleeping sickness," Felix said in a trembly voice. "And sleeping sickness can kill you," he added in an even more trembly one.

Still in the distance, but closer now, came more of those grunts.

Maisie's eyes widened.

"I thought *you* were making that noise," she said softly.

Felix shook his head, a vine dangling in his shaky hand.

"Do you think it's a hippopotamus?" Maisie asked.

"Maybe?" Felix said.

"Remember what Mr. Landon said? That they're the most dangerous animals in Africa?"

"Uh-huh," Felix said, trying to calm himself so he could get Maisie out. But his hands shook so much he had to quit and sit on them to make them stop.

Maisie wriggled a bit and her left arm came free.

She wriggled a bit more and her left leg came free, too.

"Pull," she told Felix, offering up her arm and leg.

"You don't understand how steep the ground is," he said. "If I stand up, I'll slide all the way down."

"Pull," she said, gritting her teeth.

Felix knew this was one of those times that he could not win. So he got to his knees, one leg already sliding out from beneath him. Quickly, he grabbed on to a vine. It slipped through his hand as he fell back even more.

Once again, he climbed back to Maisie, holding

on to whatever he could find, his hands burning from the vine whipping through them.

When he reached Maisie again, he tried not to say *I told you so.*

"See?" he said, which he knew meant the same thing.

"Plant yourself against that tree," Maisie said, pointing with her chin. "And then pull."

It took more crawling to get to the tree, and then a lot of slippery maneuvering before Felix had his back supported against the tree's trunk in such a way that he could lean forward and take Maisie's hand without sliding down the hill again.

But finally he did it.

He reached forward as far as he could, barely able to grasp Maisie's fingers. He held on tight. He pulled.

All of Maisie except her right foot sprang free.

"Aaarrgghh!" she said, collapsing in frustration.

Felix crawled back to his sister, and the two of them slowly unraveled the vine that still held on to Maisie's ankle.

"It's like Mom's knitting," Maisie said with a weak smile. "Remember?"

"I was thinking the same thing!" Felix said.

Their shared memory gave them renewed energy and in a few more minutes they had managed to free Maisie's foot, too.

If they could have, they would have jumped for joy.

But any movement sent them sliding. So Maisie gave Felix a light high five, and then they sat still, gazing upward, trying to figure out how to make it to the top without falling all the way to the bottom.

"Um," Felix said, his voice cracking.

"What?" Maisie said, her brows wrinkled the way they always did when she was thinking hard.

"Um," Felix said again, blinking and pointing.

"What's the . . . ," she began.

But then she saw exactly what was the matter.

Standing no more than twenty feet away, staring at them, was a family of big black gorillas.

"Don't move," Maisie whispered.

As if I could, Felix thought. He tried to remember everything he knew about gorillas. They lived in Africa, so he and Maisie had definitely landed in Africa. Something needled at him, something he was forgetting. But Felix ignored it. When five gorillas were standing this close, there was no need to worry over something forgotten. *Gorillas,* he reminded himself. *What do I know about gorillas?* They were endangered. But of course, not here in this place at this time.

The gorillas peeled bark off trees, examined it in their very humanlike hands, then ate it. One burped. One farted.

Despite herself, Maisie giggled.

Felix glared at her, like a warning.

She turned her attention back to the gorillas.

Each of their faces looked different, just like people's do. One gorilla had a thoughtful expression, another seemed happy. The third gorilla had the face of an old man, and the fourth seemed bored. The fifth . . . the fifth wore a cocky expression that reminded her of an older boy who had lived near them on Bethune Street. The boy's name was Ethan, and he used to ride his skateboard up and down the neighborhood like it was the easiest, coolest thing ever. He wore bright orange shoes made out of plastic. Once Maisie asked him about those shoes and he'd said, as if she was the dumbest person on the planet, "They're skateboarding shoes."

The cocky gorilla stopped eating bark and turned his big, cocky face toward Maisie and Felix.

To Felix, it seemed like the gorilla tilted his head and stared right at them. Felix gulped. No matter how hard he tried, he could not remember anything else about gorillas. They lived in Africa. And they were endangered. That was it. He couldn't remember if they were dangerous, like hippopotamuses. He couldn't remember if they were carnivores. Nothing.

"He acts like that kid, Ethan," Maisie said out of the side of her mouth.

"Ssshhh," Felix hushed.

"The skateboarder," Maisie added.

The gorilla took a few steps toward them, then stopped.

Stop talking! Felix told his sister silently, hoping mental telepathy might work.

"Doesn't he?" Maisie said. "Not just his expression, either. His *face* looks like Ethan."

Apparently, she had forgotten to be quiet altogether because she was talking in her regular tone of voice.

And the gorilla was walking toward them again.

The gorilla did not speed up or slow down. He

just kept moving toward them with his big gorilla steps, his gorilla arms swaying as he moved, just like a cartoon gorilla.

The other gorillas kept eating bark and scratching themselves, and burping and passing gas. The old-looking one leaned against a tree, folded his arms across his hairy belly, and went to sleep. Immediately, he began to snore. Loudly.

And the gorilla that looked like Ethan the skateboarder kept moving toward Maisie and Felix, his head bent quizzically.

Felix, already sweating in the oppressive jungle heat, began to tremble.

Maisie, however, was not afraid. As the gorilla got closer and closer, excitement swelled in her. She had never seen a gorilla before, not even in the zoo. And now she was almost ready to touch one, although she figured that probably wasn't a very good idea.

"Don't make eye contact," Felix whispered, his voice dry and cracked.

"Why not?" Maisie asked.

The gorilla stopped and looked at her, frowning.

Maisie grinned at him. His fur was coarse and

black, but his stomach was pink and the hair on his back was tipped with silver.

Felix noticed these things, too. He noticed that the gorilla's face looked like a rubber gorilla mask and that his black eyes looked like a person's eyes peering out through a Halloween mask. Then he remembered one more gorilla fact: Silverback gorillas acted like teenagers. Big and playful and, Felix thought as he sized up this silverback gorilla, probably weighing seven or eight hundred pounds. He could crush them. Easily. He could knock them out or knock them down or just about anything.

Go away! Felix thought, trying mental telepathy again. *Go away!*

But the gorilla did just the opposite. He took several bounding steps forward, and came to a stop just three feet from Maisie and Felix.

"Cool," Maisie said as soft as an exhalation of breath.

The gorilla reached forward and touched Maisie's hair with one long, gray finger.

Felix wondered if he might actually faint for the first time in his life.

The gorilla wrapped a wavy strand of Maisie's

hair in his finger. He paused. Then he pulled it, hard.

"Ouch!" Maisie said and, without thinking, she slapped his hand away.

He stepped back, startled.

For an instant, Felix thought the gorilla might walk away. The silverback shook his head and started off in the direction of the jungle.

"I can't believe a gorilla pulled your hair," Felix whispered, his voice full of fear.

"I can't believe a gorilla pulled my hair, either," Maisie said, her voice full of wonder.

Felix looked out of the corner of his eyes. Relieved, he did not see the gorilla.

"That was awesome," Maisie said. "Wait until I tell Hadley."

Hadley! That was what was needling at Felix's brain. *The Ziff twins!*

Maisie and Felix seemed to remember them at the same time. They looked at each other.

"Uh-oh," Maisie said.

The sound of footsteps pounding toward them from behind echoed through the air.

Felix started to turn to see what it was, but before he could make sense of the blur that was the silverback, the gorilla was right at Maisie's back. He made a fist and punched Maisie right between the shoulder blades, hard.

Felix heard himself yell his sister's name as she flew through the air and landed face-first on the jungle floor.

Felix ran toward her, but the gorilla ran faster. Felix watched as the silverback picked up Maisie in his mighty, hairy arms, held her tight, and ran.

CHAPTER 5

LAME DEMON

Foolishly, futilely, Felix shouted at the gorilla's hairy back: "Put her down!"

There was nothing to do except run after them. Slipping and sliding down the embankment, Felix made his awkward way in the direction the silverback ran. Hanging on to vines and branches, Felix took slow steps, glancing up every now and then to be sure he still had the gorilla—and Maisie—in his sights.

Eventually, the ground flattened out enough for him to move faster. But then he found himself in large muddy puddles, and he began to slip and slide in the muck. The puddles were strange shapes, flat and wide with funny scraped marks at the top.

Staring down as he lifted one foot after the other through the deep mud, Felix paused.

These weren't puddles.

He bent and studied the shape.

They were footprints.

Hippo footprints.

Maisie knew she should be scared. A gorilla had punched her in the back, sent her flying through the air, then picked her up from the jungle floor and was at this very minute running away with her. Even one of these things should be enough to scare the heck out of her. But somehow, Maisie felt calm.

The gorilla stunk. Worse than the monkey house at the zoo. Worse than almost anything she'd smelled. Like a million skunks spraying, plus a million gym socks, plus a million classrooms of sweaty kids. Her father always told her to breathe through her mouth when something around her smelled bad, so Maisie did that, opening her mouth and breathing in and out, in and out. The gorilla had slowed down. But he did not loosen his grip on Maisie.

"Where are you taking me?" Maisie asked him.

He glanced down at her, gave her a smug look, then just kept walking.

As he made his way along the hippo tracks, Felix kept the gorilla in his sights. It seemed like he had been walking forever. His legs ached from gripping the slippery ground so hard for so long. He was sweatier than he'd ever been in his whole life. And he wanted nothing more than a big glass of cold water back in the kitchen at Elm Medona.

Ahead on the path, Felix saw a big branch blocking his way.

Great, he thought miserably. *Just great.*

Now he was going to have to lug that thing into the brush, and maybe lose Maisie and the silverback.

With a sigh, he bent to try and pick it up. And just as he did, the branch moved.

Felix gaped at the thing.

It wasn't moving really. It was . . . slithering.

Felix took a step backward.

He was inches away from an enormous snake! So enormous that he couldn't even see its head, just what seemed in that moment like miles and miles of snake, slithering across the path.

His mind began to list all the kinds of snakes he knew lived in Africa: black mambas and boomslangs and wasn't there something called a puff adder that was the most poisonous snake in the world? Back in third grade, Maisie had written a report on deadly snakes and she'd given him nightmares by describing just how venomous certain ones were. Her favorite one was the boomslang, whose venom affected your blood's ability to clot. It could take hours for the symptoms to appear, and then you bled to death from every orifice. Felix shivered despite the heat.

The snake in front of him was the color of the ground, spotted tan and white. He closed his eyes and forced himself to concentrate on the pictures in Maisie's report. The boomslang, he remembered with relief, was green. Bright green. But his relief disappeared when he remembered that black mambas weren't actually black. Felix took several more steps backward. If a black mamba encountered prey, Felix knew it would strike as many as twelve times. He could almost hear Maisie telling him how each bite delivered enough cardio- and neurotoxic venom to kill a dozen men within one hour. *Isn't that cool?* she'd told him before shutting off the light and going to sleep, leaving Felix alone in the dark to contemplate all the terrible snakes out in the world. Like the one right in front of him. Without antivenom, he thought, the mortality rate for a black mamba's bite was 100 percent.

There were all kinds of vipers, too, he suddenly recalled with a sickening feeling. And cobras. And puff adders, he reminded himself. They could kill a grown man with just one bite. And Felix wasn't a grown man; he was just a twelve-year-old kid. How fast would a puff adder's venom kill a twelve-year-old kid?

Felix squinted at the snake. It was hard to make out against the ground because it blended in so well. The puff adder had such good camouflage, Felix knew, that people often stepped on it. The picture from Maisie's report popped into his mind. Felix took a deep breath and then another, trying to calm himself. Because he was certain that snake in front of him was indeed a puff adder. By now, it was almost all the way across the path. But wouldn't it hide in the brush there and get him when he passed by? Some of the snakes were aggressive, and others only bit when provoked. Felix was too scared to sort out their personalities right now. Besides, how did he know what provoked a snake? Why, he could be provoking it just by staring at it.

He watched as the last of the snake disappeared. But even with it off the path, he was too scared to continue. Instead, he stood paralyzed in the hippo tracks. When he looked away from where the snake had been, Felix realized that Maisie and the silverback were nowhere in sight.

With surprising gentleness, the gorilla put Maisie down and walked away.

Maisie sighed. In no time, Felix would get here and the two of them would figure out what to do next. They would find the Ziff twins and Dr. Livingstone and maybe even Amy Pickworth. They would give the map of the Nile to Dr. Livingstone and explain themselves to Amy Pickworth and then they would go home, safe and sound, just like they always did. Until then, she just had to wait.

She would sit on that big boulder over there and do just that, she decided. She would wait and not worry because somehow things always worked out. The boulder was covered with a fine red dust.

When Maisie swept her hand across the rock to brush it off, the dust took off in every direction. She jerked her hand back and peered at the tiny red dots spreading across the boulder.

Fire ants!

"Yuck!" Maisie said, shaking her hand in case even one tiny ant was still on it.

Well, she decided, she would just stand up and wait for Felix then. She fixed her eyes in the direction from which she'd come, expecting to glimpse him at any minute.

Maisie waited and waited, but no Felix.

She tried not to think about him getting eaten by a lion, bitten by a snake, or charged by a hippopotamus.

At one point, she even called his name, extra loud. But she didn't even hear her own echo in response.

A watched pot never boils, her mother had told Maisie too many times. But maybe she was right. If Maisie looked away, Felix would most definitely show up. After all, she thought as she swung her gaze in the opposite direction, she'd been down that same path and hadn't seen any lions or snakes or hippos or anything dangerous. He was just being his usual slowpoke self.

Even though the gorilla had carried her far, the jungle here looked exactly like where they'd been. Trees thick with foliage that formed a canopy of leaves above her. Branches and vines everywhere. Some dark shapes in the distance, probably even more trees.

Maisie stared harder.

Those dark shapes were moving.

Toward her.

These dark shapes were also gorillas, she realized, recognizing their distinctive swaying arms and purposeful strides. At least a dozen gorillas. And they were walking right toward her, the silverback in the lead.

Felix waited until he thought ten minutes had gone by, then he waited for what he thought was another ten minutes, then another ten, before he finally ran down the path. When he reached the place where the snake had been, he held his breath, ready for those giant fangs to dig into his leg at any second. He was well past that spot before he finally exhaled and slowed down.

But there was no time to relax. As soon as he realized he hadn't been bitten by a poisonous puff adder, he immediately began to worry over how he would ever find Maisie. If that gorilla had gone in a straight line, there was some hope. But if he turned left or right . . . well, then he could be anywhere, and so could Maisie. Even if they did move in this direction, Felix had no way of knowing if the gorilla had hurt Maisie. He could have crushed her or thrown her down or just about anything. Felix realized he was holding his breath again, and he forced himself to breathe out and then in, nice and slow, the way his mother always told him to do when he was frightened.

It felt to Felix like he'd walked forever when he finally saw fourteen gorillas up ahead standing in circle.

Felix stopped.

Now what should he do?

The gorillas looked busy. They chattered and pushed at one another, from enormous ones to three babies, all of them focused on something in the middle.

Two of the bigger gorillas stepped back from the circle, and Felix saw clearly what they were so interested in: Maisie.

He opened his mouth to shout, but then thought

better of it. What would happen if he startled so many gorillas?

Most of the gorillas were just watching Maisie, their faces filled with curiosity. But two of them were poking her with their gnarly gorilla fingers, and sniffing her. Maisie stood perfectly still.

Suddenly, one of the biggest gorillas screamed and pounded his chest and ran, fast. The others paused only briefly. They lifted their faces and inhaled. Felix watched as they went from gentle curiosity to fear. In an instant, they all screamed and pounded their chests and scattered.

Maisie's shoulders slumped with relief.

"Maisie!" Felix called, running as fast as he could toward her. "I'm here!"

When Maisie saw Felix, she burst into tears, letting herself get folded into his skinny-armed hug.

Maisie and Felix stayed like that, hugging and crying—Felix had started, too—for quite a while, the two of them sticky with sweat and tears and oppressive heat.

Finally, they calmed down and pulled apart, both of them talking at once:

"Puff adder!"

"Silverback!"

"Paralyzed!"

"Paralyzed!"

"Slithering!"

"Gorillas!"

Maisie and Felix fell silent.

"Ziff twins," Felix said.

"Uh-oh," Maisie said.

Again, they fell silent. Around them, birds cawed and leaves rustled.

"If we say . . . you know . . . we'll get out of here," Maisie said finally.

"Well, out of the jungle," he reasoned. "But not out of Africa."

"Right," Maisie said, disappointed. All *lame demon* would do is move them forward in time, not in place.

"If only we had another object," she said, thinking out loud. "Then we could go somewhere nice and safe. And cool," she added, wiping the sweat off her forehead for about the millionth time.

Next time, she decided, they would take an object that would bring them to Alaska. Maisie imagined snow and ice and cute husky dogs.

"We can't leave them here," Felix reminded Maisie.

"Well, we can't leave at all," she said.

Felix looked at her guiltily.

"Wait," Maisie said. "We can *leave*?"

Felix nodded solemnly. He reached into his pocket and pulled out the airplane compass.

"What is that?" Maisie asked.

"It's part of an airplane," Felix said. "An old-fashioned airplane. Like the *Spirit of St. Louis*."

"The spirit of what?" Maisie asked, keeping her eye on the compass.

"Lucky Lindy's plane," Felix explained.

When Maisie still looked confused, he added, "The plane Charles Lindbergh flew solo across the Atlantic."

Finally, Maisie looked at her brother, her face washed with determination.

"You mean we can get out of here and go to—"

"Little Falls, Minnesota," Felix said. "At least, that's what I'm guessing. He was born in Detroit, but his father was a congressman from Minnesota until 1917—"

"How do you know so much about this Lindbergh fellow?"

"I decided to do my aviation report on him," Felix said sheepishly. "I took a few notes."

Of course Felix already started that dumb report, Maisie thought.

"The way I see it," Felix continued, "if we say, you know"—he lowered his voice, as if Phinneas Pickworth himself might hear—"*lame demon . . .* then we're just going to go somewhere else here in Africa. But if we use this, we'll get out of here and be nice and safe in Minnesota."

Maisie nodded, considering this escape plan.

"Without the Ziff twins," she said evenly.

"Without the Ziff twins."

Maisie thought some more.

"I don't have the map for Dr. Livingstone," she said finally. "Do you?"

Felix shook his head. "I only have this," he said, holding up the compass.

"So, technically, we wouldn't be abandoning the Ziff twins," Maisie said. "Because one of them must have the map."

"Yes, but—"

"Amy Pickworth is their great-great-grandmother, right? They should be the ones to find her."

"I don't know, Maisie. What if—"

"They'll find her and give Dr. Livingstone the map and have a great adventure," Maisie said with a finality that concerned Felix.

"I really don't think we should leave them here. Snakes and gorillas and tsetse flies and hippos—"

Maisie held up her hand to shush him.

"No, Maisie," Felix persisted. "We have to think this through—"

"Sssshhh!"

Felix followed her gaze to some distant point.

"Is it them?" he asked eagerly. "Do you see Hadley and Rayne?"

Maisie's eyes widened. Her mouth opened as if she might speak, but no words came out. Instead, she lifted one quivering finger and pointed.

At first, Felix didn't see anything. But even so, he'd quickly learned here in the jungle just how good camouflage was. That snake had blended right in with the path he'd been walking on. He knew that if he looked hard enough, something would emerge up ahead.

No sooner did Felix have that thought, then the foliage seemed to move.

He blinked.

Indeed, he could make out a shape now.

Felix gulped.

"Maisie?" he whispered. "Is that a—"

Maisie nodded.

When she spoke, her voice came out hoarse and raspy.

"A lion," she managed.

Now Felix could clearly see the lion's tawny fur, its long, hard muscles.

And the lion could see him, too. It stopped and lifted its nose to the air.

Maisie and Felix held their breath.

The lion opened its mouth, revealing large yellow fangs, and let loose the loudest, scariest roar either of them could ever have imagined.

Maisie grabbed Felix's hand just as the lion lowered its head, set its golden eyes right at them, and pounced.

CHAPTER 6

THE LOUISIANA PURCHASE EXPOSITION

Felix squeezed his eyes shut, preparing for those fangs to rip into his flesh.

Instead, he felt himself being lifted off the ground, up, up, up. The wind blew as he somersaulted and the smells of all those now familiar things, like Christmas trees and cinnamon, surrounded him.

When he opened his eyes, he saw Maisie's grinning face tumble past him.

Then: nothing.

Until they dropped.

At first, Maisie saw nothing but smoke. She coughed and rubbed her eyes, wrinkling her nose at the smoke and other strange odors that filled the air. Instinctively, her hand went to the thread around her neck.

The shard was gone!

Panicked, Maisie's fingers fumbled with the thread. In the tumble it had come undone and the shard had slid off. Maisie looked all around. But the shard was nowhere to be found. How would they get back without it?

The smell of meat cooking filled Maisie's nose, distracting her. She had to squint through smoke to see anything at all. For a moment, she thought they had somehow landed back in Hawaii at the birth of Liliuokalani. She saw thatched huts and people who, with their black hair, bare chests, and loincloths, looked very much like the native Hawaiians she'd met then. They stood around a fire where a small animal was being cooked in a deep pit, talking in the strangest language she'd ever heard. Instead of the lilting syllables of Hawaiian, these people spoke in a series of rhythmic, rapid clicks.

One thing was for certain: This wasn't Minnesota. Or Hawaii, Maisie decided as she studied the faces of the people around the fire. The language was different, and their faces had a different shape than the native Hawaiians. No one noticed her. They were too eager for their dinner. To Maisie, that dinner looked very much like . . . She waved her hand to clear some of the pungent smoke clouding her vision. Her stomach rolled. That dinner seemed to be a dog, she realized. The smell of that meat and all of the smoke choked her and before she could stop herself, she threw up.

As soon as she did, everyone stopped clicking and turned toward Maisie, who had dropped to her knees and was now clutching her stomach and throwing up again. She gulped for air, trying to settle her stomach. Something caught her eye. Something white with a small blue flower on it.

The shard!

Phew! Maisie thought as she scooped it up and carefully slid it back on the thread, making sure to triple-knot it this time.

From one of the huts, a woman ran out. She wore a white cotton blouse over a sarong and a heavy, intricately beaded necklace. Her dark hair was piled on top of her head. Maisie couldn't tell if the woman was angry or worried, but her face was creased with some emotion.

"How did you get inside?" the woman said in perfect English as she kneeled beside Maisie.

Still nauseated, Maisie just shrugged.

The woman offered Maisie cold water from a small cup made out of a coconut shell. Maisie sipped it gratefully.

"Are the people already lined up?" the woman asked her.

Maisie tried to make sense of what she was being asked, but couldn't.

"Where am I?" Maisie asked the woman.

The woman smiled. "Ah! You don't even know which exhibit this is, do you?"

Exhibit? Maisie thought, but before she could say anything, the woman continued.

"This is the Philippine village," she said as if that explained everything. "We are the Igorots."

"Uh-huh," Maisie said, struggling to make sense of this new information.

"Are your parents outside?"

"Yes," Maisie said. After all, her parents *were* outside. Whatever "outside" meant.

The woman patted Maisie's arm. "It is easy to get lost, isn't it?"

"Oh yes," Maisie agreed.

From the distance, Maisie heard Felix shout: "There she is!"

At the sound of her brother's voice, Maisie felt immediately better.

"This is my brother," she told the woman, who had turned toward Felix's voice.

"What in the world . . . ," Maisie began, for once again she could not believe what she saw.

Felix was walking toward her, flanked on each side by one of the Filipino natives. Except, the man and woman were only about two feet tall. And even more strange, they were dressed like a bride and groom.

"That is Juan de la Cruz and his sister, Miss Martina," the woman explained. "They were born in the village of Tanlalgan in Capiz, a province of our country. Their parents, their three brothers and sisters, all of them are normal size. But these two are the smallest adults alive in the world."

"Wow," Maisie managed to say.

"These little people have everything we have. Every limb and muscle and bone and organ." The woman smiled. "Although they may be more intelligent than some of us. They speak three of the dialects of the Philippine languages: Tagalog, Visayan, and Pampangan. And Spanish and English."

As the trio approached, Maisie stood on her

wobbly legs, towering over Miss Martina and Juan. Still, she reached out, shook their hands, and said, "Pleased to meet you." Juan's hand was so small that it felt like a little boy's. He appeared to weigh no more than fifteen pounds. But when he spoke, his voice was as deep as a man's.

"We found your brother wandering the village," he said, smiling.

Maisie glanced at Felix, who had a bewildered look on his face.

"Yes, Juan," Maisie said. "Felix tends to wander."

Felix looked even more bewildered.

"How do you know his name?" Felix asked Maisie.

"She told me," Maisie said, cocking her head toward the woman. "And his sister is Miss Martina."

Miss Martina chuckled. "People always think we're married to each other," she said. "What a relief for someone to know our true relationship. In fact," she added with a twinkle in her eye, "his wife, Gregoria, is as tall as you."

"Really!" Maisie said.

"Wait a minute," Felix said. "Are you actually having a conversation with them? I don't get it."

Maisie rolled her eyes. "Of course! Why wouldn't I? You're the one just standing there, being rude."

"Rude?" Felix said, exasperated.

The woman who had helped Maisie smiled. "Would you like Miss Martina and Juan to lead you out of the exhibit?"

Maisie waited for Felix to answer.

"Well?" she said after he just stood there, staring stupidly.

"Well, what?" he demanded.

"What is wrong with you?" Maisie asked him. "Should Miss Martina and Juan get us out of here? Even though we don't know what's on the other side of that fence?"

Felix's gaze followed where she was pointing. A wooden fence lined the periphery beyond the thatched-roof huts.

"I mean," Maisie continued in a lower voice, "I don't know why she keeps calling this an 'exhibition.' Do you?"

"How do you know what she calls it?" Felix shrieked.

"Because I'm paying attention, unlike some people!"

"Wait," Felix said more calmly. "Beyond that fence there's a big building with a white roof. Almost like a mansion or a museum or something. Look."

Maisie stared harder.

"You're right," she agreed.

"What did you say she calls this place?" Felix asked.

"An exhibit," Maisie said. "You'd know that if you just listened to her."

Again, bewilderment washed over Felix's face.

"It doesn't seem possible," he said slowly. "But do you think these people are in a zoo?"

"*People*? In a *zoo*?" Maisie said dismissively. "No, I do not think they are in a zoo."

"Would you like to eat with us before you leave?" the woman asked Maisie. "You must be hungry."

Maisie was in fact very hungry.

"What . . . what is that you're cooking?" she asked.

The woman smiled again. "Dog," she said as if that were the best possible answer.

Maisie's stomach lurched and for an instant she was afraid she was going to throw up again.

"No," she said. Then she remembered to add, "Thank you."

"Now what's wrong?" Felix asked her, seeing her face grow pale.

Maisie sighed. "I don't want to eat roasted dog. Do you?" she said, frustrated.

"Dog!" Felix repeated, his eyes wide.

"What is wrong with you?" Maisie asked him again. "Didn't you hear her? She invited us to eat that dog they're roasting over there."

"How do you know that?" Felix said, equally as frustrated.

Maisie studied her brother's confused face.

"You really can't understand her?" she asked him.

"How could I understand a bunch of clicks?" he said, throwing his arms up. "And more important, how can you understand them?"

"I . . . I don't know," Maisie said. "But they are all speaking in perfect English."

"No they aren't," Felix insisted.

The woman touched Maisie's arm. "The exhibition is opening soon. If you aren't staying, then it's best that Juan and Miss Martina escort you back out before the crowds arrive."

"All right," Maisie said.

The woman looked at Felix sadly.

"Such a shame your brother doesn't speak Tagalog like you do."

"Tagalog? I don't speak Tagalog!" Maisie said, suddenly as confused as Felix.

Miss Martina waved her arm at Maisie and Felix.

"This way," she said.

And a baffled Maisie and Felix followed Miss Martina and Juan through the Philippine village to a large gate.

"Good-bye!" Miss Martina and Juan said.

"Thank you," Maisie said—in English.

They seemed to understand her because they answered, "You're welcome. Enjoy the Exposition!"

Maisie and Felix stood outside the gate, watching as it closed.

"Did you understand what she said?" Maisie asked her brother.

He shook his head. "Unlike you, I don't speak Tagalog."

Before Maisie could puzzle over this new strange turn of events, a little girl eating an ice-cream cone walked by with her parents and little sister. She was about six and had strawberry blonde hair and a face sprinkled with freckles.

She looked right at Maisie and Felix, took a big lick of her ice cream, and grinned a gap-toothed grin.

"This is *ice cream!*" she said as if it was the most marvelous thing in the world.

"I know," Maisie answered grumpily.

"You don't have to be so rude," the girl's mother said. "Maybe you've been here long enough to taste it, but this is her first-ever ice-cream cone and she's excited."

With that, the woman said to her daughters, "Come on Meelie, come on Pidge. Some people can try to ruin even the most perfect day."

As the family walked away from them, the freckle-faced girl turned around and stuck her tongue out at Maisie. Then she broke into a fit of giggles and skipped to catch up with the rest of her family.

"Imagine never having ice cream until you're six years old?" Felix said.

Maisie brightened.

"You understood all of that?" she asked him.

Felix scowled at her. "Well, I do speak *English*, you know."

"I don't know where we've landed," Maisie said with a sigh. "But it's definitely someplace very strange."

Felix agreed. He took a moment to look around and try to figure out where this strange place might be. What he saw puzzled him even more.

In the distance, a very tall clock stood. Its face and even the numbers appeared to be made out of flowers.

Above everything loomed a Ferris wheel, maybe the biggest Ferris wheel Felix had ever seen.

But if they were at an amusement park, why were all those Philippine natives fenced in?

As if she read his mind, Maisie said, "Remember when we met Harry Houdini? The freak show?"

Felix nodded. "Do you think that's what that village is? People go in there to gawk at everyone?"

"Maybe," Maisie said. "Let's walk around and try to find out."

They headed off in the direction of the Ferris wheel. The crowds grew thicker as they walked. The women they passed wore dresses with lots of ruffles and flounces and oversized floppy hats. The men sported summer suits, bow ties, and straw hats. The clothes were different enough that Maisie decided it had to be later than the 1890s when they'd been to Coney Island and met Harry.

"Imagine!" Maisie overheard a woman say, "Iced tea! Who would have ever thought to drink tea over ice?"

"As for me," her male companion said, "I found what they call a 'club sandwich' to be perhaps the most delicious sandwich I've ever eaten. Toasted bread, turkey, more toast, lettuce and tomato, more toast, and bacon with mayonnaise!"

"Where did you get that?" the woman said as if he'd just described the most remarkable thing. "I ate a spread made out of ground peanuts that I didn't care for. So thick!"

"Ground peanuts?" the man repeated, surprised.

"Are you listening to these two?" Maisie asked Felix.

"Where are we that introduces food like this?" Felix wondered out loud.

"And *when* are we that iced tea and club sandwiches and peanut butter are new to people?"

"And ice-cream cones," Felix said, remembering the little girl.

"Well," Maisie said, "maybe we're in Minnesota, after all. Maybe Minnesota didn't get regular food until later than everybody else."

"Maybe," Felix said, even though he didn't believe that for a second. Why wouldn't Minnesota have ice-cream cones when every place else did?

"We should keep an eye out for Charles Lindbergh, right?" Maisie asked eagerly.

"Right," Felix said, scanning the crowd as if Lindbergh might be somewhere nearby.

Maisie noticed that many people held maps, which they checked frequently.

"Excuse me," Maisie said to two women who stood side by side in pale, ruffled dresses, each studying a map. "May I take a look at one of those, please?"

"It is confusing, isn't it?" the woman in the white dress said as she handed Maisie her map. "We're on the Plaza of St. Louis, that I know for sure because there's the statue of St. Louis of France right over there."

"Uh-huh," Maisie said, trying to make sense of this information.

Felix pointed to the heading at the top of the map.

"The Louisiana Purchase Exposition," he read out loud. "We're in Louisiana?"

The woman in the white dress laughed.

"The exposition is celebrating the one hundredth anniversary of Thomas Jefferson's vision of a continental United States by purchasing the Louisiana Territory."

Her friend, a confection in pale yellow ruffles, added, "And to honor Lewis and Clark's journey west."

"Okay," Maisie said, frustrated. "We're not in the Philippines. We're not in France, even though that statue is of some guy from France. And we're not in Louisiana even though the name of this . . . exposition . . . is the Louisiana Purchase."

The women laughed.

"Stop teasing us!" the one in yellow scolded playfully. "You know you're in St. Louis, Missouri, at the 1904 World's Fair."

Maisie and Felix looked at each other, their hearts sinking.

"Missouri?" Felix said. "Not Minnesota?"

"Silly!" the one in yellow laughed.

"Let's go to the Palace of Transportation next, Myrtle," the other one said.

She glanced down at Maisie and Felix and her map.

"They have all one hundred and forty automobiles that have been driven to the fair under their own power in there," she told them.

"Under their own power?" Maisie asked. "What does that mean?"

"It means a man got into one of those automobiles and drove it here!" the woman exclaimed.

Maisie and Felix looked at each other.

"Okay," Maisie said.

"They drove from as far away as Chicago!" the woman said.

When Maisie and Felix didn't look impressed, she added, "And Philadelphia! And Boston!"

"Wow," Felix said, to be polite.

"Harumph," the woman said, taking back the map. "Considering that just last year someone drove an automobile all the way across the entire country, *I* find it impressive that all of a sudden men are driving them everywhere."

With that, she and her friend started down the six-hundred-foot-wide plaza.

Maisie peered at the monument that rose at the other end. One hundred feet high, a winged sculpture sat on top of a big globe. On a hill at that end, people streamed into a building with a giant, gold-leafed dome.

"Let's go down there and see what's going on," Maisie suggested.

But before Felix could reply, a group of teenagers rushed by them, shouting: "Geronimo! Geronimo!"

One of the boys paused long enough to grab Maisie's arm.

"He's on display in the Ethnology Exhibit!" the boy said excitedly. "Autographs are only ten cents!"

Maisie let herself get swept up in the group of teenagers.

Reluctantly, Felix followed, trying to figure out how Geronimo, the famous Apache war chief, could be on "display." After Maisie and Felix had met Crazy Horse, Felix had read a lot of books about Native Americans. He knew that Geronimo had led fierce attacks in the West after soldiers killed his mother, wife, and children. Eventually, he'd surrendered and became a prisoner of war for the rest of his life. Were prisoners of war on display here? Felix wondered.

Soon enough, they arrived at a giant tepee. In front of it sat a very old man with a face almost as wrinkled as Penelope Merriweather's. He had on a baggy black suit and a black fedora, but he was posing with a bunch of arrows pressed across his chest. Photographers snapped his picture, but his expression stayed completely stoic, with no hint of emotion. Felix suspected that if this old man was Geronimo, he must feel humiliated to have to sit there like that and have everyone gawk at him and take his picture.

"He doesn't look fierce at all," one of the teenage girls said, disappointed.

"Well, he's old now," Felix said.

The girl sighed and got in the line waiting to buy Geronimo's autograph. "I guess I'll get his autograph, anyway," she said.

"Do you think he's an imposter?" her friend asked.

The girl shrugged. "General Christiaan de Wet was much more impressive," she said.

"Was he one of the soldiers who made Geronimo surrender?" Felix asked.

The girls laughed.

"Twice a day over in the Anglo-Boer War Concession they reenact major battles from the Second Boer War," one of them explained. She had fat brown banana curls that bounced when she talked.

Felix made a mental note to look up Anglo-Boer War when he got home. He had no idea what that war was.

"It takes about three hours," her friend continued, "but it's worth it."

"They have more than six hundred veterans from both sides doing the reenactments," the other girl said, growing excited as she talked and sending her banana curls into a frenzy. "But at the very end, Boer General Christiaan de Wet escapes on his horse and leaps into a pool of water from fifty feet high!"

"Maybe not fifty feet," her friend said. "But very, very high." She sighed. "It's very dramatic."

Felix stood on tiptoe, trying to catch a glimpse of Maisie. There she was, right at the front of the line, talking to Geronimo.

When she turned to leave, she scanned the crowd until her eyes settled on Felix. Maisie waved a piece of paper and pushed her way to her brother.

"I got his autograph," she said proudly.

The two girls Felix had been talking with asked to look at it, but Felix thought the whole spectacle was terrible.

"Honestly, Maisie," he said. "How could you? The poor man is being treated like an animal in the zoo. Just like those people in that Philippine Village."

"No," Maisie said. "He's making lots of money selling autographs and photographs."

She pointed at a teenage boy walking by, smug beneath a black hat just like Geronimo's.

"He even sells his hats," she said. "He's getting rich!"

"I bet they don't even let him keep the money," Felix said.

"Who's they?" Maisie asked, tucking the autograph into her pocket.

"The US government!" Felix said. "He's a prisoner of war!"

Maisie glanced over at Geronimo carefully signing his name for someone.

"He doesn't look like a prisoner of war," she said.

"Well, he is!" Felix insisted.

"Fine!" Maisie said, exasperated. "Let's go see something else."

"Maybe Charles Lindbergh is in that fancy building over there," Felix said, trying to be hopeful.

"Is Missouri anywhere near Minnesota?" Maisie asked, wishing yet again that she'd paid more attention in social studies class. All those *M* states mixed her up.

"I don't think so," Felix said. He tried to picture the map of the United States, but the middle was just a big blank to him.

By the time they reached what turned out to be Festival Hall, the crowd had entered and the massive doors had been shut. But the sounds of a band made their way outside.

A man in a bowler hat grinned.

"Why, that's the March King himself playing 'Stars and Stripes Forever,'" the man said to no one in particular.

"Who's the March King?" Maisie asked him.

The man seemed surprised someone had heard him.

"Oh, pardon me for marveling out loud. But I can't help myself. It's all so . . . so marvelous!"

He held out two cold bottles of Dr Pepper.

"Have you had this yet?" he asked Maisie and Felix.

And even though their mother warned them to never ever take something from a stranger, the heat of the day and the fact that they'd had nothing to eat or drink in almost forever made them both eagerly accept the cold sodas.

"Isn't it delicious?" the man asked, awestruck. "Cherry soda! It goes especially well with hot dogs. I'd read about hot dogs, of course, but here there are hot dogs everywhere!"

"There are?" Maisie asked, glancing around hungrily.

"Why, you haven't tasted one yet?" the man said. "We must remedy that. Right over there that cart is selling hot dogs!"

Maisie and Felix followed the man and happily let him buy them each a hot dog. Somehow, Felix thought, this man was going to lead them to Charles Lindbergh.

"Yesterday," the man continued as if Maisie and Felix were old friends, "I heard Scott Joplin play 'The Entertainer' in there. And now, today, John

Philip Sousa. It was worth every penny to come here. Every single penny."

He added under his breath, "Despite what my father-in-law had to say about it."

"Did you come here from Minnesota?" Felix asked.

But the man shook his head. "Atchison, Kansas," he said. "You two?"

"Newport, Rhode Island," Felix told him, half expecting a reaction to this information.

The man let out a low, impressed whistle, and Felix brightened. Now the connection to Lindbergh might somehow become clear.

But all the man said was, "That's quite far!"

After she finished her hot dog in three quick bites, Maisie stopped paying attention to the man. The sight of cascading water across from Festival Hall had caught her interest and she began to walk toward it, Felix hurrying to catch up with her.

"It's beautiful," Maisie murmured as she stared out at a lagoon filled with gondolas, swan boats, and dragon boats all decked out with flowers and flags.

"The Grand Basin," the man said.

Why in the world had he followed them over here? Maisie wondered.

"At night it's lit with more than twenty thousand lights," he continued, his voice filled with awe.

"You aren't Mr. Lindbergh by any chance," Felix blurted. "Are you?"

The man shook his head. "You're looking for this Lindbergh fellow, are you?"

"I think so," Felix said.

"If he's performing—" the man began, but he got interrupted by a woman rushing up to him.

"Well, there you are," the woman scolded.

Maisie looked up into a vaguely familiar face. Where had she seen this woman before?

"Daddy," a little girl eating an enormous cone of cotton candy said. "Taste this!"

That little girl, Maisie realized, was the freckle-faced kid from before, the one with the ice-cream cone.

The girl's mother recognized Maisie, too.

"Let's go see Lincoln's log cabin, Sam," she said to her husband. "The girls have been asking all afternoon."

Her husband let some cotton candy dissolve on his tongue, his eyes rolling heavenward as he did and a small moan of pleasure escaped his lips.

"What is this sugary delight?" he asked.

"Cotton candy," Felix told him.

"Cotton? Candy?" the man said, obviously displeased by the name.

Meelie scowled at Felix.

"No it isn't," she said with a small stomp of her foot. "It's fairy floss, Daddy."

Her father grinned. "Yes! Yes, it *is* fairy floss."

"Sam?" his wife said impatiently. "Lincoln's log cabin?"

"Of course," Sam said affably.

He glanced at Maisie and Felix.

"Have you two seen it yet? The log cabin where Abraham Lincoln was born? They brought it here all the way from Kentucky!"

"No, we—" Maisie began.

"I'm sure their parents will take them at some point," the woman interrupted.

She gathered her own two little girls and nudged them forward. As Felix watched her acting so motherly, he ached for his own mother. But Maisie only noticed how oddly the little girls were dressed. Instead of the froufrou the other little girls here wore, these two had on strange, navy-blue, one-piece bloomers that reminded Maisie of the uniforms some schools made girls wear for gym class.

"What weirdos," she whispered.

The one called Meelie turned around, her face sticky with cotton candy.

"Fairy floss," she said, sounding triumphant.

Maisie and Felix watched the family get swallowed up by the crowd.

"Now what?" Felix asked, dispirited.

"Lame demon?" Maisie suggested.

"Stars and Stripes Forever" played its final notes. A bell in the Floral Clock tolled.

And Felix sighed.

"Lame demon," he said.

CHAPTER 7

STARGAZING

Maisie gazed up at an inky sky filled with twinkling stars. She had landed on soft grass and, from what she could tell, in someone's backyard. To her right stood a white house, to her left a shed, and, all around everything, a picket fence.

Crickets chirped. From somewhere nearby came the quiet laughter of children followed by deeper, adult tones. Even though she couldn't see anything clearly, this place felt homey and familiar.

Felix's voice cut through the warm night air.

"I feel like we've landed smack in the middle of America," he said.

Squinting, Maisie could see that the lump across the lawn was actually her brother.

"Me, too," she said. "It feels nice here."

The children grew excited, and Maisie stood and moved toward the shed, Felix close behind her.

"Up there," Maisie whispered, pointing to the roof.

Two girls sat perched on the roof with their parents, all of them gazing at the starry sky.

"Are you sure we'll see one?" one of the girls demanded.

"If you're patient and keep still," her mother said.

"Just don't fall off the roof, Meelie," her father said, and the other little girl laughed.

"It's not funny!" the girl called Meelie said.

"Your sister was inspired by that roller coaster in St. Louis," the father said.

"St. Louis!" Maisie blurted.

Felix clapped a hand over her mouth to silence her.

"I applaud your spirit of adventure, Meelie," the mother said kindly. "You know that."

"I do, too," the other girl said. "You built that ramp all by yourself, and you were brave enough to get in that wooden box and ride it right off the roof—and you didn't even kill yourself!"

"Not bad for such an exhilarating experience," their father said.

Meelie sighed. "It felt just like flying," she said wistfully.

Felix tugged at Maisie's arm and pulled her around the corner of the shed.

"That's the same family we saw at the World's Fair!" he whispered.

"What? You mean that bratty kid with the cotton candy?"

"Yes. I remember her name was Meelie because that's such a funny name. And the sister is called Pidge," Felix said.

Maisie nodded. "That's right."

They both turned their gaze upward.

"That means one of those kids is who we need to give the compass to," Felix said, disappointed.

"No, Charles Lindbergh," Maisie agreed. "Or any of my aviatrixes for that matter."

"There's nobody named Pidge or Meelie in Mom's room, is there?" Felix asked.

"Not that I know of."

Meelie and Pidge began to shout.

"Look! Look!"

Maisie and Felix stepped away from the shed to get a better view of the sky. Something bright white appeared in the sky, and just like the fireworks on the Fourth of July it seemed to explode and then fall toward them.

"Oh no!" Felix shouted. "Is it a meteor? Is it crashing?"

He ducked his head and covered it with his arms, as if that might actually protect him. Hadn't a meteor destroyed all of the dinosaurs?

With all of the excitement, the family on the roof didn't seem to hear him. They were all too busy shouting and jumping up and down.

Maisie grabbed Felix's arms and pulled them away from his face.

"Look," she said, her voice so filled with wonder that Felix had no choice but to look up.

"They're shooting stars," Maisie said, awestruck.

"Wow!" Felix said. "Cool!"

Both children stood, staring up as another star shot from the sky.

"How come we can't see these at home like this?" Maisie wondered out loud.

"Light pollution," Felix said.

From the roof, the father's said, "Well, girls, did you make a wish?"

"I wished that someday I get to ride a star across the sky!" Meelie exclaimed.

"SSSHHHH!" Pidge reprimanded. "You're not supposed to say your wish out loud, Meelie. It won't come true."

Their parents chuckled.

"I don't think even Meelie will be able to lasso a shooting star and take it for a ride," their father said gently

"What a night," her mother said with a sigh.

Pidge yawned.

"Bedtime," her mother said reluctantly. "There are some nights, like this one, that I wish could last forever."

"Me, too, Amy," the father said. "Me, too."

Maisie and Felix pressed themselves against the back of the shed so that the family wouldn't see them when they climbed off the roof. Meelie jumped down first, followed by Pidge, and then the parents came down more carefully.

Maisie watched as the father took the mother's hand in his, and she leaned her head against his shoulder and they watched their daughters run ahead, up the stairs and into the perfect white house.

"A family," Maisie said sadly.

"We're a family, too," Felix told her.

"A broken one," she said.

And they both stared at the parents walking hand in hand across the grass and inside.

The shed was unlocked, so Maisie and Felix went inside it to sleep. The shed, Maisie thought, looked like a perfect shed. Rakes and hoes lined one wall. A big, silver watering can sat beside burlap bags of soil. Trays on a counter had seeds just beginning to sprout. Against another wall, a snow shovel leaned and four pairs of snow boots stood—two children's, a woman's slender pair, and a large men's pair. Under the window, tools glinted in the moonlight, saws and hammers of all sizes and screwdrivers and tools that Maisie didn't even recognize.

She dipped her hand into a bucket of nails and let them run through her fingers. Then she lifted her hands to her nose and inhaled the sharp metal smell on them. In the corner, she saw fishing poles, small ones and long ones.

"I think we've landed in the most perfect place in the world," she said wistfully.

Felix had found some sleeping bags and he unrolled two.

"Come on," he said, patting one of them as he unzipped and climbed into the other. "We should get some sleep. Who knows what tomorrow is going to bring?"

Reluctantly, Maisie agreed.

But when she got into her sleeping bag, she couldn't fall asleep. Her mind was too full of things. First, there were the weddings. Great-Uncle Thorne's and her father's. How she wished her family had stayed together, that there was no wedding to Agatha the Great, that Penelope Merriweather didn't want to get married so old. Then there was the play. Her excitement about getting the lead didn't quite assuage her stage fright. Finally, there was being here. Where were they? And who was Meelie or Pidge?

Maisie sighed and closed her eyes. Already, Felix was breathing softly beside her, asleep.

But almost immediately her eyes popped open.

The Ziff twins! Where are they? And are they all right?

She shivered remembering the gorillas and the lion.

"Felix," she said to her sleeping brother.

"Mmmmm," he murmured.

"Felix!" she said louder.

Felix mumbled and turned over, away from her.

How can he sleep when so many things are happening? Maisie thought.

She poked Felix until he swatted her hand away and grumbled, "What?"

"The Ziff twins," she said.

Felix rubbed his eyes and struggled to sit up. "I know," he said, feeling guiltier than he'd ever felt in his life. "I know."

"I was so afraid back in Africa," Maisie said, "all I could think about was getting out of there. But now that we're here and safe . . ."

She couldn't say it out loud, but she didn't have to.

"They might be dead!" Felix blurted.

"Or worse," Maisie added.

"What's worse than dead?"

"I don't know. Mauled by that lion or held captive or a million terrible things," Maisie said.

"Stop!" Felix groaned.

"Of course, it's possible that they're okay," Maisie offered.

"Sure," Felix said, unconvinced.

"It's possible that they found Dr. Livingstone and gave him the map and are back in Newport already," she continued.

As she spoke, that possibility seemed more likely.

"Yeah," Maisie continued, nodding as she spoke, "that's what happened. For all we know, they even met Amy Pickworth! In fact, I bet they did!"

Feeling much better, Maisie snuggled back into the sleeping bag. Felix was going on and on about how *un*likely that was and how the Ziff twins might even have malaria or some other disease.

"Uh-huh," Maisie said, certain that the Ziff twins were home in their beds.

The next thing she knew, sunlight streamed in the shed's window and it was morning.

Felix stretched and unzipped his sleeping bag.

"I'm going to peek outside," he told Maisie.

Slowly, he pushed the door open.

Out of nowhere, the biggest, shaggiest dog he'd

ever seen jumped on him, knocking him backward.

Felix yelped in surprise.

The dog began to lick his face.

"Yuck!" Felix said.

"A dog!" Maisie shouted happily. She ran over to Felix and the dog and petted the big, shaggy thing.

"What's your name, buddy?" she cooed.

"His name is James Ferocious," came a girl's voice from outside the shed. "And at my command, he'll bite your head off."

Maisie and Felix peered outside.

The freckle-faced girl called Meelie stood there in blue jeans with the cuffs rolled up, a red-and-white-checked shirt with the sleeves rolled up, and a straw hat over her pigtails. She was chewing on a piece of grass and studying them as hard as they studied her.

"I think your dog is actually very friendly," Maisie said. "He wouldn't bite us, even at your command."

"Don't test that theory," Meelie said.

Pidge's head popped out from behind Meelie.

"Did you sleep in the shed?" she asked in disgust.

"Yes," Felix admitted.

"But why?" Pidge asked, coming out from behind her sister. She was dressed identically, except her shirt had blue-and-white checks. "Why would anyone sleep in a shed?"

"We . . . um . . . ," Felix began, glancing over at Maisie. But Maisie was completely mesmerized by James Ferocious.

"Are your parents somewhere else?" Pidge continued.

"Yes!" Felix said. "Exactly!"

Pidge nodded solemnly. "Like when we stayed in Kansas, and Mama and Papa came here to Iowa," she said to Meelie.

"Iowa," Felix said to himself. Another one of those big states in the middle. He vowed to memorize every one of them when he got home, right after he looked up the Anglo-Boer War.

"But we stayed with our grandparents. Not in a shed by ourselves," Meelie said, keeping her eyes on Felix. "Where're your grandparents, boy?"

"Dead!" Felix announced.

"Oh," Pidge said. "That's sad." She patted his arm sympathetically.

It was already clear to Felix that these two sisters were very much alike. Except that Meelie was obviously the leader, and Pidge her follower. Kind of like him and Maisie, he thought uncomfortably.

"So your parents are—" Meelie began.

"Somewhere else," Felix said.

Meelie narrowed her eyes. "And your grandparents are—"

"Dead," Felix said, nodding.

"And you two are just—?"

Felix shrugged. "For the time being, anyway."

"Meelie," Pidge said in her solemn voice, "I want to keep them. Can we? Please?"

Meelie seemed to consider this.

"I bet they're more fun than Laura and Ringa," Pidge offered.

Meelie studied Maisie and Felix. "You think? I'm not so sure."

"Well, these two are *real* and Laura and Ringa are make-believe—"

"They're invisible," Meelie corrected. "Not make-believe. There's a difference."

"These two are visible," Pidge pointed out.

"True," Meelie said, twirling that blade of grass. She was silent for a moment more.

"Boy," she said finally, "what's your name?"

"Felix. Felix Robbins. And that's my sister,

Maisie, who's fallen in love with your dog."

"Felix," Meelie repeated.

"Robbins," Felix said again. "And Maisie Robbins."

"Well, Felix Robbins, we want to keep you," Meelie said.

Pidge shrieked with delight and clapped her hands together.

"Thank you, thank you, thank you!" she shouted, hugging her sister around the waist.

"That's great," Felix said. "Thanks. I guess."

Actually, he felt a little weird, like he was a prisoner or something. Felix thought of Geronimo, forced to sign autographs and have his picture taken while he was a prisoner of war.

"Did you see Geronimo at the fair in St. Louis?" Felix asked Meelie, because she seemed to be the one in charge.

Meelie frowned. "Who said we were at the fair in St. Louis?" she asked him.

"Uh . . . you said it, didn't you?" Felix stammered.

Thankfully, Pidge said, "We did see him! Papa bought one of his hats! And Mama said to stop spending money and Papa said you only get to the

1904 Louisiana Purchase Exposition once in a lifetime and you have to enjoy it and then he said, 'Amy, stop sounding like your father,' which is our grandfather and he disapproves of almost everything Papa does."

"That's enough, Pidge," Meelie said sternly, and went back to studying Felix.

"You like fishing?" Meelie asked him finally.

"I never tried," he said.

"You've never gone fishing?" Pidge said in disbelief. "Why, we always go fishing, don't we, Meelie? We go almost every day and we catch perch, and Mama cleans them up and dips them in eggs and cornmeal and fries them with potatoes and Meelie always eats a bowl of radishes with that dinner but of course she eats radishes with *everything*. You love radishes, don't you, Meelie?"

Felix listened in wonder. Pidge could talk without taking a breath longer than anybody he knew.

"Do you like adventures?" Meelie asked, like it was a dare.

That got Maisie's attention.

"We have adventures you wouldn't even believe," Maisie told her.

"Oh yeah?" Meelie said.

"She built a roller coaster and rode it off the roof," Pidge said, excited and proud. "And she didn't even die! She just tore her dress and got a bruise on her face and split her lip—"

"I got kidnapped by a gorilla," Maisie said.

"You did *not*," Meelie said dismissively.

"And I survived a fire at sea and—"

Pidge pointed a finger at Maisie and grinned.

"You're funny," she said. "You're a storyteller, which is different than a liar, but not much."

"It's true!" Maisie insisted.

"Our mother was the first woman to climb Pike's Peak," Meelie said, placing her hands in her hips. "In 1890."

"Which is a real adventure, and a real accomplishment," Pidge said. "And Pike's Peak is in Colorado, and it's more than a fourteen-thousand-foot-high climb."

"Wow," Felix said, impressed. "That's something."

Meelie chewed on the blade of grass and studied Maisie.

"Let's go fishing," she said at last.

By the time Maisie and Felix and Meelie and Pidge and James Ferocious made it to the banks of the Des Moines River, Maisie and Felix had learned practically everything about them from Pidge. Except who they were and why one of them should get the airplane compass.

"We were both born in Atchison, Kansas," Pidge told them. "Meelie's two years older than me and our grandfather Otis is a lawyer and our father is a lawyer but not such a good one, we are practically in financial ruin," Pidge said with a dramatic sigh.

"Grandfather Otis does not approve of many things we do," Meelie added. "He wants us to wear dresses instead of bloomers. He wants Father to get a better job."

"He didn't even want us to go to the World's Fair in St. Louie," Pidge said. "He said it was a waste of money!"

"When really it was the most wonderful experience of all of our lives," Meelie added dreamily. "We stayed with our Otis grandparents back in Atchison for a whole year while our parents set up the house here in Des Moines. We were finally reunited last year," she added happily.

Before Felix could comment, Pidge started up again. "Our mother teaches us at home so we get to play all the time and make up games and go fishing."

"I'm exceedingly fond of reading," Meelie said. "Pidge is not so fond of it."

"So am I!" Felix said.

"Have you read a hundred books?" Pidge asked him. "'Cause Meelie has."

"I also keep a scrapbook of newspaper clippings," Meelie continued. "I collect stories about women who got successful doing men's things, like directing movies or working in advertising or running businesses or even mechanical engineering. Or even," she added, "being a lawyer!"

"Our mother's a lawyer," Maisie said.

Meelie stopped walking and scowled at Maisie. "She is not!"

"Yes, she is. She works at Fishbaum and Fishbaum," Maisie said.

"Hmm," Meelie said, and started walking again.

"Is she successful, though?" Pidge asked. "Like Grandfather Otis? Or more like Father?"

"I think somewhere in between," Maisie said.

The Des Moines River appeared over the next hill, wide and glistening in the sunlight.

Meelie led them to the spot she said was best to catch perch, and without hesitation took worms from a can she'd brought along and stuck them on the fishhooks at the end of each line.

"If we catch enough for dinner, Mama will fry them up for us," she said, handing first Maisie and then Felix a fishing pole.

"There's nothing like fried perch," Pidge said happily.

Meelie unfolded a handkerchief and set it on the grass.

"Snacks," she said, pointing to the red radishes there.

"Meelie loves radishes! I told you so!" Pidge said.

Felix wrinkled his nose at the radishes and the worms wiggling at the end of the lines and the smell of wet dirt and river water that filled the air. Maybe Maisie thought this was the most perfect place in the world, but Felix wasn't so sure.

He watched as Pidge took her thumb and pressed the line right above the reel against the fishing pole. Then she flipped something on the reel. And without letting go of the line, she pulled the pole back and cast out.

Felix watched as first Meelie's, then Pidge's line seemed to fly far out over the river. They reeled them in just enough to keep the line snug.

"Why are you two just standing there?" Meelie asked Maisie and Felix.

Slowly, Maisie tried to imitate what Pidge and Meelie had done, but her line flopped like a cooked noodle and fell right at her feet instead of anywhere near the river.

Felix didn't even get that far. When he pulled the pole back, the line dropped behind him, too.

Meelie laughed, hard.

"Just keep practicing," she said.

Maisie's face set with determination. She tried again and again until finally, triumphantly, her line dropped into the water.

"There," she said, satisfied.

Felix tried just as many times, but the line tangled or drooped or went nowhere at all.

And everyone, including Maisie, ignored him.

Maybe, Felix thought, if he stood on one of the rocks in the shallow part of the river, when his line didn't cast far enough, it would still drop into the water at least.

"So," he said, trying to sound casual, "I'm going down there to fish."

The three girls kept their eyes on the water and their own lines, waiting for a nip or tug.

"Yup," Felix said. "I'll be down on those rocks."

"I got one!" Maisie shrieked as her line bent into an arc.

Meelie grinned and guided her, telling her to stay calm and do this and that. Felix had stopped listening and instead made his way down the embankment to the river. There, he stepped onto the first rock, surprised by how slippery it was.

Well, he thought, *it* is *in the water. Of course it's slippery.*

Slippery, and too round to stand on, he decided. He took a tiny jump onto the next rock.

"Yikes!" Felix screamed. This rock was not only slippery, it was more slippery than the first one.

Felix struggled to keep his balance and not drop the fishing pole at the same time.

But he failed at both.

The pole dropped with a splash into the river.

And Felix's feet slipped out from beneath him, sending him into the water with an even bigger splash and a loud grunt.

The weight of his clothes and his shoes kept him from popping back up, and Felix found himself fighting to get to the surface. The water was murky. Slimy, green weeds surrounded him and wrapped their long tentacle-like arms around his legs. There really were a lot of fish in this river, Felix realized as lumpy, brown fish and tiny silver ones swam by.

Pushing upward with all his might, Felix finally broke the surface of the water.

But once he did, he saw that the current was much faster than it appeared from the land and he was being rapidly swept downriver. In the distance, he saw Maisie, Meelie, and Pidge, unaware that he was even gone and growing smaller and more distant by the second.

"Help!" he called to them, but his voice was gobbled up by the roar of water somewhere ahead.

Felix tried to grab on to a rock that jutted from the water, but he moved past it too fast.

"Help?" he tried again, even though he couldn't even see the girls anymore.

His feet kicked against the weeds and muck below, while his arms dog-paddled to keep his head above the water.

What in the world is that sound? Felix wondered as the roar became louder and nearer.

He craned his neck, but all he could see was more river up ahead.

The water around him started to get frothy. And, he realized, it was swirling like the water in a whirlpool.

Felix blinked.

"Help!" he called again, now moving his arms and legs even faster in an attempt to fight the current.

The current that was pulling him straight into the fastest-moving rapids Felix had ever seen.

That roar was the rapids rushing and swirling.

And no matter how hard Felix fought, the rapids were winning.

CHAPTER 8

FIRST FLIGHT

The rapids grabbed on to Felix and threw him around hard. He felt like laundry in the washing machine getting bounced and tossed, the water everywhere, churning all around him. He knocked into rocks. He banged against pieces of wood floating past. Holding his breath for so long made his chest ache and burn.

Just when he thought he had to give up, that his lungs would burst if he didn't get air, the rapids lifted Felix up and spat him out.

He landed in shallow water, on his back, with a thud.

Gasping, Felix let his exhausted body sink into the muddy bottom. The river water, calm now, spilled over him in gentle ripples. But the sound of the rapids still roared in Felix's ears, mixing with the sounds of his own panting.

A pigtailed shadow fell over him.

"What are you doing all the way down here?" Meelie demanded.

Felix could only shake his head and swallow more air.

"Don't tell me you don't know how to swim, either?" Meelie asked, disgusted.

"I. Can. Swim," Felix managed to get out.

Meelie looked past him, toward the thundering rapids. Then her gaze settled back on Felix, her eyes widening.

"Did you just go down Dead Man's Leap?" she asked.

Perfect name for it, Felix thought as he nodded his reply.

"You must be the bravest boy in the world," Meelie said, plopping down in the mud and water right next to him. "I admire bravery," she said. "Like my mother climbing Pike's Peak."

If he could have found his voice, Felix might have told Meelie that it was stupidity, not bravery, that brought him to Dead Man's Leap. And sheer luck that got him through those rapids.

"Someday I'm going to do something brave and the whole world will know about it," Meelie said.

She was maybe the most confident person Felix had ever met. Even more sure of herself than Bitsy Beal. And kind of a braggart, too. But she was so cute with those freckles and that big, toothy smile, that Felix almost didn't mind her boasting.

Meelie leaned close to him, like she was about to tell him a secret.

"Do you think you almost died in there?" she asked, her voice soft.

"Felt. Like. It."

Meelie's eyes sparkled. "Someday I'll do something brave and almost die, and then I'll tell everyone how I survived."

Felix took a big breath. Finally, he seemed to have enough air in his lungs.

"Did you catch any perch?" he asked, his voice hoarse.

"We did!" Meelie said. "Lots!"

She stood, reaching her hand down to help Felix to his feet.

He let her pull him up out of the muck, and held on to her as they walked along the river, his knees still shaking from his time in Dead Man's Leap.

"This," Meelie announced, "is our museum."

Maisie sighed, unimpressed.

In three large jars on a table at the end of the porch were bugs of some kind. She and Felix had been in Des Moines for almost a month and the perfect Midwestern life Maisie had envied when they first arrived had grown dull. Sometimes, Meelie hitched James Ferocious to a doll carriage and made him walk around the neighborhood, Pidge running ahead of him with bones to keep him moving. Sometimes, they went fishing for perch. Sometimes, they played elaborate games that Meelie invented. There was nothing wrong with any of that, but there wasn't anything especially exciting, either.

"These are very rare moths," Meelie said in a hushed voice. "Luna. Regal. Cecropia."

Felix let out a low whistle. "Cool," he said.

Meelie smiled at him. With her shiny, white teeth and all those freckles, Felix thought she was one of the cutest girls he'd ever met. He didn't know many girls as brave or adventurous as Meelie. She didn't hesitate to put a worm on a hook or pick up a garter snake and examine it closely. *Let's try!* seemed to be her favorite thing to say. And she read everything. At night, she came into the shed with a flashlight and books for her and Felix and they lay side by side reading while Maisie grumbled about wanting to go to sleep.

"I bet you found those yourself, didn't you, Meelie?" Felix asked admiringly.

Maisie rolled her eyes. "It's not such a big deal to find moths," she said. She'd seen dozens of them sticking to the screen door almost every night.

"It's a big deal to find these three kinds," Meelie said.

"Right," Maisie said, "they're very rare."

"They are!" Pidge said. "Meelie looked them up in the encyclopedia and it said in there that these are very rare moths."

"I think they're . . ." Felix struggled for an adjective that Meelie would like. "Impressive!" he said.

Just then, Meelie's mother called to them from the kitchen. She had no idea that Maisie and Felix slept in the shed every night and assumed they were neighborhood kids. All she ever said was how glad she was that Meelie and Pidge had made some friends.

The four children walked through the big parlor with its fancy couch and chairs. The couch had lace doilies on the back that Meelie called "antimacassars." *Fancy word for doilies,* Maisie had said, and Meelie explained that "macassar" was a pomade men wore in their hair and *anti*macassars kept the stuff off the upholstery. Now, every time they walked into the parlor Felix said that word to himself.

It was so much cooler in the house that Maisie would have been happy to stay indoors. But Meelie liked being outside, so outside they stayed. If Pidge complained she was hot and wanted to go inside, Meelie scolded her. "Pidge, it's summer! You'll wish we could play outside once winter comes and then it will be too late!" Through the dining room with its heavily polished table, was a large vase of fresh flowers in the center flanked by heavy silver candlesticks, and a high china cupboard filled with fancy dishes and serving pieces.

Then into the kitchen, where Meelie and Pidge's mother stood over a freshly plucked chicken.

She didn't look up when they entered, but started to talk to them right away.

"I was just about to cut up this chicken and I realized what a good science lesson it would be to have you watch."

Meelie and Pidge stood on either side of their mother, peering at the chicken with wide-eyed curiosity. But Maisie and Felix held back. The kitchen smelled mostly of the apple pie Meelie and Pidge's mother had just baked, but behind the apple and cinnamon smell came the faint odor of blood. *That chicken has just been killed,* Felix thought with disgust.

"Look how beautifully her little lungs fit above her little heart," their mother said as if she were looking at a piece of art. "Isn't she lovely?"

"Yes, Mama!" Pidge said enthusiastically. "She's a beauty!"

"Does our heart fit over our lungs like that, Mama?" Meelie asked, pressing her hand to her chest.

Her mother nodded, pleased. "Exactly, Meelie. Who knew we could learn so much from Sunday's supper?"

"Speaking of Sunday . . . ," Meelie began.

Her mother pretended to look confused. "Tomorrow? That Sunday?"

"Don't tease!" Meelie said.

"What's happening tomorrow?" Maisie asked. *Maybe something interesting,* she hoped.

"Something really, really great," Pidge said, grinning.

"We're going to the state fair!" Meelie announced happily. "Mama, can we take Felix and Maisie with us?"

"I don't see why not," her mother said.

The state fair? Maisie thought. She imagined pigs and cows and pie-eating contests, none of which sounded the least bit interesting.

Felix loved the fair. He loved all the animals with their big, blue ribbons. He loved all the farmers with their vegetables—corn and giant tomatoes and deep orange carrots with the greens still on. He loved the women standing proudly beside their homemade pies, a dizzying array of lattice and double crusts, berries and cherries and custards, streusel toppings, and shiny pecans or walnuts.

But Maisie thought it was boring to look at smelly animals or stare at a bunch of food you couldn't even eat. Plus, the day had gone from very warm to hot, and the fairgrounds offered little shade. And all Meelie and Pidge wanted to do was ride the merry-go-round, again and again, changing which brightly painted horse they sat on each time.

She was relieved when the girls' father showed up and asked them to come with him.

"I have the most amazing thing to show you," he said.

"But I still haven't ridden on the white horse," Pidge complained. "Or the purple one!"

Her father laughed and tugged on one of her braids. "This is so much better than that purple horse, Pidge. I promise you."

Still, Meelie and Pidge kept finding things to distract them from whatever their father was trying to show them.

"*Real* ponies!" Pidge said, pointing to two tired-looking Shetland ponies. "Can we, Papa?"

Her father glanced up at the sky where dark gray clouds had started to roll in.

"The thing is, if we don't get there before the rain

comes, you'll miss this marvelous invention," he said.

"What is it?" Maisie asked, eager to see something marvelous and amazing.

Their father turned to her, his eyes shining with excitement. "An aeroplane," he said, awed. "It's an amazing new invention that Orville and Wilbur Wright flew for the first time five years ago out in Kitty Hawk, North Carolina."

Disappointed, Maisie shot a look at Felix. But he didn't seem to notice.

"How something heavier than air can fly . . . well, that baffles me," Meelie's father continued.

"Just one ride on a pony?" Pidge pleaded. "Then we'll go see your flying machine."

Reluctantly, their father let them take a ride around the corral on the ponies. But when Pidge and Meelie begged for another ride, he refused.

"Look at those storm clouds," he said.

He led them to the edge of the fairgrounds. A field with a high wire fence around it and a higher wooden fence inside that had a big sign in front of it: FLYING AEROPLANE.

Again, Maisie tried to catch Felix's eye. Were they really going to spend the rest of the day looking at an airplane? Felix either didn't see her or chose to ignore her as Meelie found yet another distraction.

"Paper hats!" she shouted.

"Oh!" Pidge said, jumping up and down. "I want the yellow one!"

Maisie followed everyone to the booth selling the ridiculous paper hats, which were really just circles of cardboard covered with paper flowers. They tied under the chin with colorful ribbons. Once that rain started, those hats would dissolve into lumps of wet paper.

Meelie and Pidge tried on one hat after another as their father paced impatiently.

"That one looks pretty on you, Meelie," Felix said.

"It looks like you have an upside-down basket on your head," Maisie said.

"Well, I like it," Meelie decided. "I think I'll wear it every day until I'm ninety-nine years old."

Her father quickly paid for the hats and told his daughters, "Not one more delay, girls. You are going to see this aeroplane, and you are going to thank me profusely once you do."

Without anymore complaining or stopping, they

entered through the fence and stood in the field.

"*That's* the airplane?" Maisie said, staring in disbelief at the thing in front of them.

It did have two wings, but one was stacked on top of the other. Instead of a shiny plane with the name of an airline painted in bright colors on the wing, this thing was made of wood and wire. It barely looked like it would hold together if it could even take off. In the middle of the plane, between the wings, a man wearing goggles and a leather cap sat on a seat, the engine right behind him. Maisie narrowed her eyes. The tail of this "aeroplane" looked more like a box kite than a real plane's tail.

The engine sputtered to life. Another man, dressed exactly like the one inside the plane, turned a wooden propeller until it spun on its own.

"Now watch," Meelie's father said quietly. "It's going to fly."

Slowly, the plane rolled across the field.

"I don't think that thing can fly," Maisie said, just as it began to rise up into the air.

Meelie gasped.

They all watched as the aeroplane circled the field.

"They'll never be used for much," Meelie's father said. "But they're still quite an invention."

"I think they'll carry people all over the world," Maisie said. "And cargo, too."

Meelie's father laughed. "That's a funny idea, Maisie."

"Papa!" Meelie said, watching the aeroplane land. "I want a ride in it!"

"Do you think they'll let us?" Pidge asked.

"I don't know," their father said, "but we can find out."

"With those clouds," the man who had started the propeller told them, "it's probably not a good idea to go up."

They all turned their eyes upward.

"They do look ominous," Meelie's father agreed.

"The ride only takes a few seconds," Meelie reminded him.

"Well," he said, considering.

"You couldn't pay me to go up in that thing," Maisie said, staring at the contraption.

"I thought they were going to carry people all over the world," Meelie's father teased.

"Bigger ones," Maisie said. "Aluminum ones."

He laughed. "Big aluminum aeroplanes! I like that!"

"It's true," Maisie said under her breath.

Felix glared at her. And this time, Maisie pretended not to see him.

"I'll take the three big kids up," the man said finally. "For five dollars."

"Five dollars!" Meelie's father said. His hand went instinctively in his pocket, but he didn't take any money out.

"I want to go, too," Pidge whined.

"If it hasn't started to rain," the man said, "I'll let you and the little girl go up free of charge."

Their father looked longingly at the aeroplane, then slowly nodded.

"Don't tell your mother that I spent part of her grocery money on a few seconds in a flying machine," he said.

Meelie whooped. "Now this is an adventure!" she shouted.

"Pidge can take my place," Maisie said, staring at the plane. That wire and wood looked like it could break apart easily.

Felix had the very same thought. But he didn't

want Meelie to think he wasn't brave, so he kept it to himself.

Meelie spun around to face Maisie, who was lagging behind as they crossed the field to the plane.

"Why are you so afraid of everything?" she said angrily. "If you don't take chances, nothing wonderful will ever happen to you."

"I take a lot of chances," Maisie said, remembering how it felt when she first stood on that stage for the audition. She'd thought she might faint from fright.

"Then stop complaining and let's fly," Meelie said.

"Okay," the pilot explained, "what's going to happen is you three will climb in, I'll start up the propeller, and I'll jump in once it gets going. Boyd's gone on home. 'Cause of the storm."

Meelie got in first, followed by a reluctant Felix and an even more reluctant Maisie.

The little seat was so tiny that they had to all scrunch close together.

"My heart is beating like a hummingbird's," Meelie said happily.

Felix wanted to say something, but fear had

lodged in his throat like a big stone and he couldn't speak.

The man warned them that it would be too noisy to speak over the wind and the engine.

"So you just need to sit back and enjoy quietly," he added, giving the propeller a spin.

"Um," Maisie said, "is that rain I feel?"

"For goodness' sake," Meelie said.

"I think I felt it, too," Felix said.

He was about to point out that raindrops splattered his glasses, but he didn't get a chance.

A gust of wind sent the propeller spinning like a pinwheel and before the pilot could jump in with them, the plane lifted up, up, up.

Meelie screamed, no longer impressed by flying.

At first, Felix thought the loud rumble he heard was coming from the engine. But then he realized it was thunder.

He clenched the steering wheel.

A bolt of lightning cracked blue across the black sky.

Rain began to fall, softly at first, then harder and harder, soaking them.

More thunder.

Another crack of lightning, closer this time.

All three children gripped the steering wheel now.

But even that couldn't stop the plane from plummeting downward, spinning toward the ground below, fast.

CHAPTER 9

AMELIA EARHART

"Do something! Now!" Meelie screamed.

Felix did do something. He let go of the steering wheel and covered his eyes. And just like he'd heard people say happened right before you died, his life flashed before him.

Almost like a home movie, he saw himself as a very little boy. He remembered the feeling of his father pushing him in a swing, the bucket kind that held you in nice and tight. They were probably at the Bleecker Street Playground, and Felix could practically feel the spring sunshine on his face, and the nudge of his father's strong hand. Beside him, his mother pushed Maisie in her own little bucket swing, but Maisie wanted out. She wanted to play in the sandbox or slide down the curly slide, and Felix could hear her young voice demanding, *Out! Out! Out!*

Then there were the four of them at Florent, their favorite neighborhood diner, and the salty taste of the skinny fries that came, improbably, with eggs. His father lifts one French fry and dips it in ketchup and feeds it to Felix's mother, who looks up at his father like she loves him.

He saw himself learning to ride a bike on bumpy Hudson Street. Running on the beach at Cape May. Petting the classroom guinea pig, Cinnamon. Whispering to Maisie in the dark in their apartment on Bethune Street. He heard the crack of the bat when he hit his first home run, his mother singing as she cooked spaghetti carbonara, the sound of his father's key in the lock when he came home from his studio.

If someone had told Felix that they'd remembered all of these things, he would have thought it took some time. But in fact, they truly flashed through his mind, like lightning bugs on a summer night.

And they stopped as soon as the plane began to gasp and burp.

Felix opened his eyes. The rain was falling steadily and his hair and face and shirt were already drenched. But, he realized with relief, the plane had leveled off.

He held his breath, prepared for the nose to turn downward again.

Instead, it began to climb again, though not at all smoothly.

They had dropped low enough for Felix to see the surprised faces of the pilot and Meelie's father and Pidge and maybe a dozen other onlookers, all standing in the rain staring up at them.

Felix's ears popped like crazy.

The wind made it hard for him to turn his head, but when he did what he saw made him yelp.

Maisie was flying the plane!

Meelie had let go of the steering wheel, too, and she sat, her face frozen in a terrified expression, her eyes wide, her mouth opened.

But Maisie looked determined. Her jaw was set and her eyes were narrowed with concentration.

The plane seemed to buck rather than fly. It ascended with a lurch, and then it dropped. Over and over again.

Meelie's face turned pale first. But before long,

her skin took on a vaguely greenish cast.

Below, the pilot waved his arms and shouted at them, though his words got lost in the noise of the engine and the loud wind and the sound of the rain hitting the plane.

"He wants me to land!" Maisie shouted above the din.

Although Felix knew they had no choice, he also knew that his sister had no idea how to land a plane.

Maisie clenched her jaw and focused on the pilot.

He was pointing to a particular spot. He was moving his arms as if to say "go slow."

The important thing, she decided, was to keep the plane straight. At first, it had seemed like a living thing—a bucking bronco, maybe, like they had in rodeos. But clutching the wheel so hard that her knuckles had turned white and pulling up on the rudder, Maisie somehow was keeping the thing straight. Kind of.

If she could manage for it to stay straight while she dropped it lower, she might be able to land the thing. Although probably not in the spot where the pilot kept pointing, ever more frantically.

"I'm landing her," Maisie said.

She said it out loud, but she was really talking to herself, as if by saying it out loud she had made a commitment.

Meelie let out a long cry: "Noooooooooo!"

Felix decided to close his eyes again.

"We're going to die!" Meelie yelled.

"Be quiet!" Maisie ordered. And for once, Meelie obeyed.

"I need you both to look out and tell me if I'm getting to close to anything," Maisie said. "I need to keep my eyes looking straight ahead."

Now Felix understood why the aeroplane was out in this field—away from the crowded fairgrounds, the rides and animals and people. And the trees that bordered the whole fair. Here, they circled the mostly empty field, and as they slowly descended, he saw the onlookers below scatter.

As Maisie set about trying to land the plane, her nerves calmed. Just like when she had finally started to speak the lines onstage at her audition, the world around her disappeared. All that mattered was keeping the plane straight and gently descending. Her whole world became that cockpit, that steering wheel and rudder, that field in front of her.

Even all the noise stopped, replaced by a quiet that seemed to come from deep inside her.

Last autumn, when a hurricane was threatening to hit Newport, Mrs. Witherspoon had told them how hurricanes were classified, how fast their winds were. She'd pointed to the very center of the picture of the swirling storm. *This is called the eye,* she'd said. Inside the eye, everything was calm, despite the violent winds that surrounded it. That's where Maisie was now, in the eye of her own storm.

"Ready," she said out loud.

"No!" Meelie screamed.

But Maisie didn't answer her. She wasn't asking Felix and Meelie if *they* were ready. She was telling herself that *she* was ready. Ready to land this plane.

The ground seemed to be coming up toward the plane, as if it wanted to grab them and toss them away. The wet, green grass looked almost close enough to touch.

Maisie kept her grip steady, though. The plane was as straight as she could keep it.

The wheels were about to touch down.

The pilot yelled to her: "Steady! Steady!"

Meelie bawled.

Felix held his breath.

The wheels kissed the ground.

Bumped up.

Came down a bit harder.

The plane began to skid on the wet grass. Maisie fought to control it, but she couldn't.

It turned in slippery circles, tipping right and then left as it did.

Just when Felix thought the plane would flip over or fall, it slowed and finally stopped. Already, everyone was running across the field in the rain. Felix watched the faces, awash with a combination of fear and relief, rushing toward them.

Meelie was the first off the plane, climbing hastily out and racing into her father's arms. Felix stood, his legs so shaky that he had to sit back down until his breath slowed and the trembling stopped. Even then, it seemed his knees might give way at any moment.

But Maisie just sat behind the wheel, looking stunned. She watched the scene unfold before her—Pidge and her father hugging Meelie, Felix standing awkwardly in the crowd, the pilot explaining aerodynamics in a very loud voice to anyone who would listen.

"It's that girl who saved them," the pilot said, pointing to Maisie.

"But how?" someone asked.

"Luck. Blind luck," someone else said.

Meelie stepped out of her family's embrace.

"I will *never, ever* get on an aeroplane again as long as I live!" she announced.

Her father tousled her hair. "You won't have to worry about that," he said. "These things are just for show, anyway."

He glanced at Maisie, still perched in the plane. "Despite what your friend Maisie thinks," he added with a grin.

Slowly, Maisie stood and climbed down from the plane. Her hair was wet and plastered to her head and face. Her feet sank into the soaked grass as she sloshed toward the others. Nothing seemed real to her. This place. The plane ride. The tailspin and her white-knuckled rescue. None of it.

Meelie stared up at Maisie with wide, admiring eyes.

"See?" she said. "You *are* brave. You can do anything you set your mind to."

Maisie nodded, letting the idea sink in.

"Maybe you're right, Meelie," she said.

"Let's get home, kids," Meelie's father said. "Get you out of these wet clothes and get some warm food into you."

Felix threw his arm around his sister's shoulders.

"You were amazing," he told her.

"I was, wasn't I?" Maisie said.

"And modest, too," Felix teased, giving her shoulder a squeeze.

"You know what?" Maisie asked. "I'm ready to go home. I think that between the gorilla and the plane, I've had enough excitement for a while."

Felix sighed. "All we have to do is find the person, give him the compass, get a lesson—"

"Stop!" Maisie interrupted. "Let's just figure it all out. Soon."

Meelie's mother had baked chicken and creamed corn and roasted potatoes waiting for dinner. And a big bowl of Meelie's favorite: radishes. She'd made biscuits, too, and she put a small pitcher of honey beside them.

"So?" she said after they all had sat down and piled food on their plates. "Was the fair exciting?"

Meelie and Pidge glanced at Maisie.

"No," Maisie said, forcing her voice to sound casual. "Fun," she added, chewing on one of the flaky biscuits. "But not exciting."

"We saw an aeroplane!" Pidge blurted.

Her father cleared his throat. A warning for her to keep their adventure to herself.

"I'd like to fly in one of those," her mother said dreamily.

"It's awful!" Meelie said fiercely. "The wind is in your face the whole time, and it's so noisy you can't even hear yourself think and then the stupid thing almost crashed."

Everyone stared at Meelie.

But it was her mother who spoke first. "You went up in an aeroplane?" she said, her nostrils flaring in anger.

"I . . . ," Meelie began.

Her mother turned to her father.

"You let her go up in one of those flying machines?" she demanded.

"Why, you just said yourself how much you'd like to fly in one!"

"Yes, but I'm a grown woman! Children shouldn't ride in aeroplanes!"

"I didn't," Pidge said quickly. "I stayed right on the ground and watched."

Her mother looked from her husband to Meelie and back again.

"It was an adventure!" Meelie's father said.

"It was terrible," Meelie said, taking another piece of chicken as if to end the entire conversation.

"Good," her mother said. "Maybe that will teach you a lesson, Miss Amelia Earhart."

Felix gasped.

"Uh-oh," Pidge giggled. "You know you're in trouble when Mother uses our real names."

"You're . . . you're *Amelia*?" Maisie sputtered. "*Earhart*?"

"What of it?" Meelie said.

Maisie and Felix broke into big grins.

"Oh," Felix said. "Nothing. Nothing at all."

Maisie poured some honey on another biscuit.

"Do you know what I think, Meelie?" she said, still grinning. "I think you will fly in an aeroplane again. And I think you'll love it."

Mr. Earhart laughed. "You certainly have a lot of predictions about these aeroplanes, Maisie."

"I did a big report on aviation in school," she said.

Mr. Earhart laughed harder. "A big report?" he said. "There's not much to say about it, is there? You've got the Wright Brothers at Kitty Hawk but not much else."

"I don't care what you say, Maisie," Meelie said. "I'm done with flying machines."

"Amelia Earhart," Maisie said smugly, "I'm willing to bet that you fly all the way across the Atlantic Ocean in an airplane. Alone!"

Meelie rolled her eyes. "I don't think I've ever heard anything more ridiculous in my entire life."

"Imagination is a good thing to have, Maisie," Mr. Earhart said. "And you certainly have a big one."

"All this nonsense does not get either of you off the hook," Mrs. Earhart said sternly. "Next thing I know, you're going to tell me you actually paid for the honor of almost getting yourself killed up there."

They all looked down at their plates.

"What?" Mrs. Earhart said. "How much?"

"When will they ever get the chance to fly in an aeroplane again?" Mr. Earhart said.

Maisie smiled at Felix but decided to keep quiet. They had found Amelia Earhart and gone on her first flight with her. Now all they had to do was give her that compass, and they would be home in no time. Maisie knew Amelia Earhart had already given her the best advice: *Be brave*. And Maisie had already taken it. She'd saved all of their lives by landing that plane. Stage fright was nothing compared to that.

CHAPTER 10

JAMES FEROCIOUS

Maisie woke up to the sound of rain on the roof of the shed. She snuggled deeper into her sleeping bag, waiting for the door to burst open and Meelie and Pidge to come in like they did every morning. But this morning would be different. Maisie would give the compass to Meelie and she and Felix would be home in no time.

No sooner did she think that, then the door burst open and Pidge ran in, alone.

"It's just terrible!" Pidge cried.

Maisie and Felix both sat up at once.

"What's happened?" Felix asked her.

"James Ferocious is sick, and Mother says we can't take him to the veterinarian because it costs too much money and Father gave all the week's money to go in the aeroplane!"

"Dogs get sick all the time, Pidge," Felix said. "Don't worry."

"But Meelie wouldn't listen," Pidge continued. "She took him to the veterinarian, anyway."

"Well then, he'll make him better," Felix said.

"But how will we pay?" Pidge sobbed. "You have no idea the money troubles we have. Grandfather thinks Father is a spendthrift and a bad lawyer and irresponsible."

"So Meelie is at the vet's?" Maisie asked, already disappointed that she would have to wait to give Meelie the compass. "When will she be back?"

"How would I know that?" Pidge said.

"It'll be okay," Felix said, patting Pidge on the back. "You'll see."

"Want to play a game or something?" Maisie asked, eager to make the time pass as quickly as possible.

"I don't think I can concentrate on a game," Pidge said, shaking her head.

Then, as if another idea had just popped into her head, she slapped her forehead.

"Back in Atchison, our neighbors had a big black dog named Magic. That dog had the very same symptoms as James Ferocious and the veterinarian put him to sleep!"

"I think James Ferocious is going to be fine," Felix said.

"Let's play cards," Maisie decided. "Do you have any cards?"

"That veterinarian back in Kansas," Pidge continued as if neither Felix nor Maisie had spoken, "he said that someday they would be able to do an operation to save a dog like Magic, but that day had not yet come."

She turned her teary face to Felix.

"What if Meelie comes back without James Ferocious?" Pidge asked him.

"Let's do something to get your mind off this," Maisie tried again.

Pidge looked at her angrily. "Do you have a dog?" she demanded.

"No—"

"Then how would you know anything about it?"

"I've always wanted a dog," Felix said. "But our mother refused."

Pidge kept her gaze on Maisie.

"I'm tired of playing with you," she said. "Where is your mother, anyway? When Meelie comes back, I'm going to tell her that I don't want you to sleep in the shed anymore."

"When Meelie comes back," Maisie said, "we're leaving, anyway."

"Good," Pidge said, crossing her arms.

"Good," Maisie said.

The rain kept falling, and Maisie, Felix, and Pidge kept waiting for Meelie to come back. Pidge sat by the window in the shed and watched for her. Maisie retrieved the compass and held on to it, ready to thrust it at Meelie as soon as she walked in the door.

It seemed to take forever, but finally Pidge shouted, "Here she comes! And she has James Ferocious with her!"

Pidge ran and opened the door, letting a very wet Meelie and James Ferocious inside.

The shed filled with the smell of wet dog, and James Ferocious set about shaking off all the rain, spraying water everywhere.

"I was afraid he was incurable," Pidge said, hugging the dog's neck.

Meelie chewed her lower lip.

"I'm afraid he is incurable," she said finally, looking longingly at the dog.

"Oh no!" Felix said.

Meelie nodded. "He has what Magic had back in Atchison," she told Pidge.

"Something called an 'obstructed bowel,'" she explained to Maisie and Felix.

Felix smiled. "They can fix that!" he said happily. "When we lived in New York City, our upstairs neighbor had a standard poodle named Gogo with an obstructed bowel, and the vet operated and Gogo was fine."

Meelie was looking at him, confused. "Maybe in New York City they can do things like that, but here in Des Moines, our veterinarian says an operation like that, on a dog, is impossible. At least in the foreseeable future."

"Oh," Felix said.

"Are you lying to me?" Meelie asked him. "About this dog, Gogo?"

He shook his head.

"You two say some very strange things," Meelie said thoughtfully.

"I'm tired of playing with them," Pidge said.

Meelie didn't respond. She just kept studying Felix and Maisie.

Felix squirmed uncomfortably beneath her gaze. "They're way ahead of the times in New York City," he said finally.

"Hmmm," Meelie said.

Maisie had been quiet up until now. But she stepped forward and rubbed James Ferocious behind the ears. The dog rested his big, shaggy head in her lap.

"What if I told you that we could bring James Ferocious home with us and save his life?" Maisie said.

"I wouldn't believe you," Meelie said, and Pidge agreed.

"The only thing is, we would have to keep him then," Maisie explained. "We couldn't return him to you."

"You want James Ferocious?" Pidge asked, offended.

"We could save his life," Maisie said to Felix.

"I'm not sure it would work," he said, even though he recognized the determined look on his sister's face. She had decided to take the dog home with them to save his life, and Felix knew how impossible it was to talk Maisie out of anything once her mind was made up.

"I think it would work," Maisie said.

"It doesn't matter," Pidge said. "You can't have our dog. Can she, Meelie?"

"Well," Meelie said, thinking. "The question is whether James Ferocious alive but far away is better than James Ferocious dying. Because the veterinarian said he would die."

Pidge's face crumpled.

"We would take very good care of him," Maisie said.

"I thought your mother refused to let you have a dog," Pidge said almost desperately.

"We haven't asked in a while," Felix admitted.

"And we have so much room where we live," Maisie added. "He could run around the grounds, and we could take him for walks on the beach."

She looked at Meelie. "He'd be happy," she said. "I promise."

Maisie took the compass from her pocket, fingering its smooth surface. "We would leave you this," she said, showing it to Meelie.

Meelie frowned. "What's that, anyway?"

"It's from an aeroplane," Felix said.

"But I don't need anything from an aeroplane!" Meelie insisted. "I'm never flying in one again!"

Maisie held out her other hand for the leash.

"Felix," she said, "maybe you should hold on to the leash, too. Just to be sure."

Felix did. He put his hand over Maisie's, which had the leash tucked into it.

"You'll take good care of him?" Meelie asked.

Maisie and Felix nodded.

Meelie leaned close to Felix and whispered in his ear. "Are you fortune-tellers or something?"

"Something like that," he whispered back.

"Here," Maisie said, offering the compass to Amelia Earhart. "Just in case you ever do fly again."

Meelie took a deep breath and cocked her head at Maisie and Felix.

"All right," she said at last, and she reached her hand out to take the compass from Maisie.

But then Meelie paused.

"Let's make a pact," she said. "The three of us."

"What kind of pact?" Felix asked.

"Let's promise to do something brave in our lives," Meelie said. "Something so brave that the whole world will take notice of us."

Tears sprung to Felix's eyes.

"Amelia Earhart," he said softly, "I think the whole world will take notice of you. But if you ever get the crazy idea to fly around the world, don't do it, okay?"

"Me?" Meelie laughed. "You don't have to worry about that. If I never see another aeroplane again, it will be too soon."

"I promise to be braver," Maisie said, already imagining what that might mean.

Felix said, "So do I."

With one of her big, toothy smiles shining on them, Meelie took the compass.

The last thing Maisie and Felix saw in 1908 was Amelia Earhart and her sister, Pidge, staring down at the compass in Meelie's hand.

The next thing Felix knew, he was back in The Treasure Chest with James Ferocious licking his face.

"He's here!" Felix shouted happily.

Maisie peeked over the dog's shaggy body, smiling.

But Felix's own smile faded quickly. He looked around The Treasure Chest, half hoping the Ziff twins were here, too, safely returned from the Congo. But the room was empty, except for Great-Uncle Thorne, who stood right where they'd left him.

"So?" he demanded immediately. "Did you see her?"

Maisie shook her head.

"Tarnation!" Great-Uncle Thorne roared, and without another word he stormed out of The Treasure Chest.

"If only Rayne and Hadley were here, too. I hope they're okay," Felix said.

"Maybe they got back sooner?" Maisie said.

Felix brightened slightly at that notion. But he deflated just as quickly.

"No," he said, thinking out loud. "If they were back, Great-Uncle Thorne would have seen them. He would have known."

Maisie and Felix let this information settle in.

"So they're still in the Congo," Maisie said hopefully.

"Let's figure out what to do next," Felix said,

taking James Ferocious's leash and walking toward the door.

"Wait until Mom sees that we brought a dog home," Maisie said.

"A dog that needs surgery," Felix reminded her.

"I think Great-Uncle Thorne will be so impressed by our ingenuity that he'll pay for the operation," Maisie said.

They walked out of The Treasure Chest, leading James Ferocious down the stairway and out into the hall, where to their surprise they walked right into their father.

"Dad!" Maisie shrieked.

Felix stared at his father, taking in his curly hair and his hands speckled with paint.

"What are you doing at Elm Medona?" Felix asked him.

Their father pointed at James Ferocious.

"What are you doing with a dog?" he asked.

"We . . . rescued him," Maisie said.

"Your mother let you have a dog?" their father said in disbelief.

"She doesn't exactly know about him yet," Felix admitted.

"His name is James Ferocious," Maisie told her father. "Isn't he beautiful?"

"He's shaggy, that's for sure," he said, bending to pet the dog's big head.

"But why are you here?" Felix asked again.

"To see you two," their father said. "And to talk to your mother," he added.

"She's been kind of upset," Maisie told him.

"I know."

"She doesn't want you to marry Agatha the Great," Felix said softly.

"Agatha the *Great*?" his father repeated.

"Oops," Felix said, turning red.

"The thing is," their father went on, "as it turns out, I'm not going to marry Agatha. The Great," he added with a small smile.

"You're not?" Maisie said, half disappointed and half relieved.

"Why did you change your mind?" Felix asked.

"I didn't. She did."

"How could she?" Maisie said in disbelief. "You're the best!"

Their father sighed. "I think it all happened too fast. The divorce and the move and Agatha and me."

"Does Mom know?" Felix asked.

He shook his head. "She's not home."

"Let's go downstairs and you can make us some normal food," Felix said. "Everything here is French."

"Happily," their father said.

Happily, Maisie thought. She liked the way that word sounded.

They were sitting in the Library eating grilled cheese sandwiches and tomato soup when their mother got home. Their father made the best grilled cheese sandwiches in the world—extra buttery and extra gooey. He also made the best tomato soup, even though it came from a can. Instead of water, he made it with milk, and he added celery salt as his secret ingredient. *Comfort food*, he always called grilled cheese sandwiches with tomato soup. Maisie wondered if her father needed comfort, if Agatha the Great had broken his heart.

The good news was that he was going to move back to New York City, anyway.

"So maybe you guys can come down every other weekend," he told them.

"That sounds nice," Felix said.

But Maisie had another thought. Maybe their father would marry their mother all over again. She didn't know for certain, but she bet that happened sometimes. People got divorced and then realized the error they'd made.

"I smell a dog!" their mother called from the hallway.

"How could she?" Maisie wondered out loud.

"A wet dog," their mother said as she came into the Library.

She looked at James Ferocious. "A very big, wet dog," she said, putting her hands on her hips.

Then she noticed their father sitting there, a half-eaten grilled cheese sandwich in his hand.

"And what are you doing here?" she said, flustered. "Shouldn't you be getting married or something?"

"That's an interesting story," their father said.

"Really? I'd love to hear it," their mother said, flopping onto one of the Moroccan leather sofas.

James Ferocious plodded over to her and dropped his shaggy head into her lap.

"Ugh!" she said. "Wet dog."

But she didn't make him move, which Maisie took as a very good sign.

"Maybe we could speak privately?" their father said.

Before their mother could answer, they heard the tap of Great-Uncle Thorne's walking stick coming down the hall.

He marched in the room and stood glaring at first Maisie, then Felix, then their mother, then their father, and finally at James Ferocious.

"Where are the Ziff twins?" he boomed. "Still not back?"

"I . . . that is to say . . . we . . . ," Felix stammered.

"And who are you?" Great-Uncle Thorne demanded, pointing his walking stick at their father.

The walking stick had an ivory horse's head with an emerald eye. That eye seemed to glare at everyone, too.

"Jake Robbins," their father said, standing and wiping his hand on his jeans before he held it out to Great-Uncle Thorne. "Their father? Her husband?"

"*Ex*-husband," their mother mumbled.

Great-Uncle Thorne reeled around to face James Ferocious.

"And what in the world is that?" he bellowed.

"Maybe we could talk in private?" Felix offered.

"Today is not a good day," Great-Uncle Thorne announced. "Penelope Merriweather got cold feet."

"She got cold feet?" Felix repeated.

"You nitwit! She backed out of the wedding!"

"She did?" Maisie said in disbelief.

"Could someone please catch me up here?" their mother said, sitting up straighter and trying unsuccessfully to move James Ferocious's head from her lap. "The Ziff twins are missing?"

"No, no," Maisie said quickly.

"Not exactly," Felix added.

"Could someone give me a straight answer?" their mother demanded.

Great-Uncle Thorne thought for a moment.

"We need to talk in private," he said, glowering at Maisie and Felix from beneath his bushy eyebrows.

Maisie, Felix, and James Ferocious got up to follow him.

But Maisie hesitated.

"Mom? Dad?" she said.

Her mother was pressing her fingertips into her temples like she had a bad headache.

"What?" her mother said without looking up.

"I think for a bad day, this is a good day," Maisie said.

She didn't wait for an answer. Instead, she ran to catch up with Felix and Great-Uncle Thorne, James Ferocious at her side.

AMELIA EARHART
Born: July 24, 1897

Disappeared over the Pacific Ocean on July 2, 1937

Declared dead on January 5, 1939

Amelia Earhart was born in Atchison, Kansas, and her sister, Grace, was born two years later. The two girls were inseparable, with Amelia the leader and Grace her follower. Their childhood nicknames of Meelie and Pidge were used throughout their lives. In 1890, their mother, Amy Otis, became the first woman to climb Pike's Peak in Colorado, and she used that sense of adventure in raising her daughters. Rejecting frilly dresses and big bows for their hair, Amy sewed them navy-blue bloomers that allowed them to climb and run and play more easily. The girls grew up climbing trees, collecting insects, and creating daring stunts for each other.

In 1907, their father took a job with the Rock Island Railroad in Des Moines, Iowa. Their maternal grandfather, Alfred Otis, who had been a judge and a successful bank president, did not support his daughter's marriage to Edwin Earhart. His concerns proved to be valid. Within five years of the move to Des Moines, Edwin Earhart's drinking became such a problem that he lost his job and the family's belongings had to be auctioned off. Amelia Earhart said that that was the day her childhood ended. The family moved to Minnesota, but when Edwin lost his job again a few years later, Amy Earhart took her daughters to live in Chicago.

Amelia's love of science eventually led her to attend Hyde Park High School, where the chemistry lab was more sophisticated than the one at her local school. Despite the strong science curriculum there, Amelia did not make friends, and that—combined with her family's reversal in fortune—made her last year in high school a sad one. The caption under her yearbook photo reads: A.E.—THE GIRL IN BROWN WHO WALKS ALONE.

When World War I broke out, Amelia trained as a nurse through the American Red Cross (which was started by Clara Barton) and volunteered at a military hospital in Toronto, where her sister lived. In 1918, the Spanish influenza became a pandemic, killing an estimated fifty million people—ten times as many people who died in the war itself. (Some estimates put the toll as high as one hundred million!) Amelia contracted influenza that November and had a long convalescence at Pidge's new home in Northampton, Massachusetts. Set to enroll at Smith College, Amelia changed her mind when she recovered and instead went to Columbia University (where Alexander Hamilton studied) to study medicine.

A year later, she dropped out of college to live with her parents, who by then had settled in Long Beach, California. Back in Toronto, Amelia had seen a World War I flying ace perform, and an earlier fear of flying and airplanes—inspired by an experience at the Iowa State Fair when she was a girl—disappeared. She later said that the airplane that day in Toronto spoke to her. But it wasn't until December 1920 in Long Beach that Amelia became determined to learn to fly. On January 3, 1921, she took her first flying lesson, and within six months she bought her own airplane, a bright yellow Kinner Airster biplane that she named *Canary*. She also bought a leather jacket that she slept in every night so that it looked broken in, and cut her hair short like the other female aviators did. This look—the worn leather jacket and short hair—became the trademark of Amelia Earhart.

Flying *Canary*, Amelia made her first women's record by flying to an altitude of 14,000 feet. But in 1924, her parents divorced and, with her mother's inheritance depleting, Amelia sold her plane, bought a yellow sports car that she named *Yellow Peril*, and, with her mother, took a six-week transcontinental car trip that ended in Boston. There, with her mother now out of money and unable to pay for her daughter's college, Amelia eventually became a social worker at Denison House. One afternoon in 1928, a man phoned her there and asked, "How would you like to be the first woman to fly the Atlantic?" Without hesitation, Amelia replied, "Yes!"

A year earlier, Charles Lindbergh had flown his solo flight across the Atlantic. Amy Phipps Guess owned a Fokker F.VII named *Friendship*, and wanted to make the flight herself. But three women had died within the year trying to be that first woman, and Guess's family objected to her taking on such a dangerous mission. Instead, she asked aviator Richard Byrd and publisher George Putnam to find the "right sort of girl" for the trip. There are many theories as to why they selected Amelia Earhart. People thought she resembled Charles Lindbergh. She had a wholesome "All-American" personality. But she was also an accomplished pilot who had logged 500 hours in the air. Whatever the reasons, she was asked to join pilot Wilmer "Bill" Stultz and copilot/mechanic Louis "Slim" Gordon.

On June 17, 1928, the team left Trepassey Harbour

in Newfoundland and arrived at Burry Port, Wales. Although she was promised time at the controls, Earhart never flew the plane during the nearly twenty-one-hour flight. Although she described the flight as a "grand experience," she later said she felt like just a "sack of potatoes." Nevertheless, reporters were much more interested in her than either of the male pilots who actually flew the plane, and the flight brought her international attention. They were greeted with a ticker-tape parade in New York and a reception held by President Calvin Coolidge at the White House. The press nicknamed her "Lady Lindy."

From then on, Amelia's life revolved around aviation. In 1931, she married George Putnam, and the two embarked on a major publicity campaign for her that included a lecture tour, a book and book promotion, and endorsements for products that ranged from luggage to Lucky Strike cigarettes. These endorsements helped her finance later flights. As an associate editor for *Cosmopolitan* magazine, she encouraged women to enter the field of aviation. In 1929, she was among the first aviators to promote commercial air travel through the development of a passenger airline service. With Charles Lindbergh, she represented an airline that later became Trans World Airlines (TWA) and she invested time and money in setting up the first regional shuttle service between New York and Washington, DC.

During all this time, Earhart and Putnam were also secretly planning her next big flight: a solo flight across the Atlantic Ocean. Such a flight would make her the second person and first woman to successfully accomplish that. On May 20, 1932, five years to the day after Lindbergh, she took off from Harbour Grace, Newfoundland, headed for Paris. But strong north winds, icy conditions, and mechanical problems plagued the flight and forced her to land in a pasture near Londonderry, Ireland. As word of her flight spread, the media surrounded her, both overseas and in the United States. President Herbert Hoover presented Earhart with a gold medal from the National Geographic Society. Congress awarded her the Distinguished Flying Cross—the first ever given to a woman. At the ceremony, Vice President Charles Curtis praised her, saying she displayed "heroic courage and skill as a navigator at the risk of her life." To Earhart, the flight proved that men and women were equal in "jobs requiring intelligence, coordination, speed, coolness and willpower," a belief she'd held since she was a young girl growing up in Kansas.

Amelia Earhart continued to break aviation records. Between 1930 and 1935, she broke seven women's speed and distance aviation records. In January of 1935, she became the first person to fly alone from Hawaii to California. That April, she became the first person to fly from Los Angeles to Mexico City. Less than three weeks later, she became the first person to fly nonstop between Mexico City and Newark.

In 1937, as she neared her fortieth birthday, she wanted a monumental, and final, challenge: to be the first woman to fly around the world. "I have a feeling that there is just about one more good flight left in my system," she said, "and I hope this trip is it." That March, she flew the first leg from Oakland, California to Honolulu, Hawaii, where it was determined the plane needed servicing. During takeoff, witnesses claimed that a tire blew. Earhart thought that either a tire blew or the landing gear collapsed. Others cited pilot error. Whatever happened, however, the plane was severely damaged.

But Earhart was not deterred from her goal.

Determined to make the flight, she had the twin-engine Lockheed Electra rebuilt. On June 1, Amelia Earhart and her navigator, Fred Noonan, departed from Miami and began the 29,000-mile journey. After numerous stops in South America, Africa, India, and Southeast Asia, they arrived at Lae, New Guinea, on June 29, 1937. At this stage, about 22,000 miles of the journey had been completed. The remaining 7,000 miles would all be over the Pacific. Frequently inaccurate maps had made navigation difficult for Noonan, and their next hop—to Howland Island—was by far the most challenging. A flat sliver of land 6,500 feet long and 1,600 feet wide, Howland Island is located 2,556 miles from Lae in the mid-Pacific. "Howland is such a small spot in the Pacific that every aid to locating it must be available," Earhart said. Unessential items were removed from the plane to make room for additional fuel. The US Coast Guard cutter *Itasca* was stationed just offshore of Howland Island, assigned to communicate by radio with Earhart and guide them to the island once they arrived in the vicinity. Two other US ships, ordered to burn every light on board, were positioned along the flight route as markers.

At midnight on July 2, 1937, Amelia Earhart and Fred Noonan took off from Lae. Despite favorable weather reports, they flew into overcast skies and intermittent rain showers. This made celestial navigation difficult. As dawn neared, Earhart called the *Itasca* and reported that the weather was cloudy. The *Itasca* sent her a steady stream of transmissions but she could not hear them. Her radio transmissions had been irregular through most of the flight, and now became faint and interrupted with static. At 7:42 AM, the *Itasca* picked up the message: "We must be on you, but we cannot see you. Fuel is running low. Been unable to reach you by radio. We are flying at 1,000 feet." The ship tried to reply, but the plane seemed not to hear. At 8:45, Earhart reported, "We are running north and south." Nothing further was heard from Earhart. Earhart's transmissions seemed to indicate she and Noonan believed they had reached Howland's charted position. The *Itasca* used her oil-fired boilers to generate smoke for a period of time but the clouds in the area around Howland Island might have prevented the fliers from seeing it. The dark shadows of the clouds on the ocean surface may have been almost indistinguishable from the island's subdued and very flat profile. Attempts were also made to reach them by Morse code, but that, too, failed.

The most extensive air-and-sea search in naval history to date began immediately. But after spending four million dollars and scouring 250,000 square miles of ocean, the United States government reluctantly called off the operation on July 19. George Putnam financed a private search that also proved unsuccessful. But the question of what happened to Amelia Earhart remains unanswered.

In 1938, a lighthouse was constructed on Howland Island in Amelia Earhart's memory. Amelia Earhart has become synonymous with aviation and with women's achievements. Across the United States there are streets, schools, and airports named after her. In a letter she wrote to her husband before a dangerous flight, she said: "Please know I am quite aware of the hazards. I want to do it because I want to do it. Women must try to do things as men have tried. When they fail, their failure must be but a challenge to others."

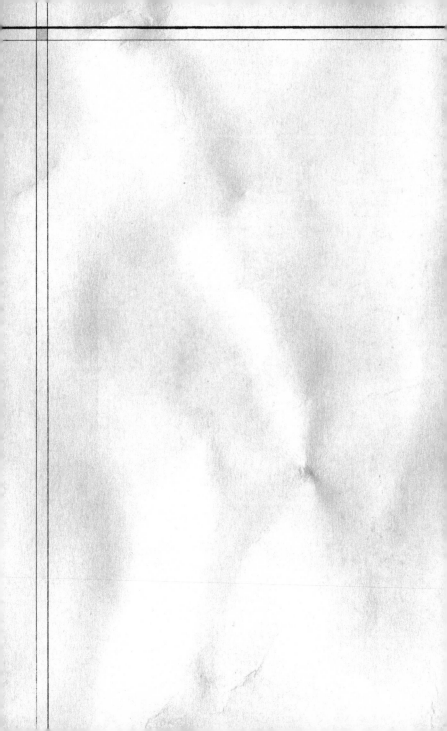

I do so much research for each book in The Treasure Chest series and discover so many cool facts that I can't fit into every book. Here are some of my favorites from my research for The Treasure Chest, No. 8: *Amelia Earhart: Lady Lindy*. Enjoy!

There are so many things that I'm excited about in book eight! First, there is Amelia Earhart herself. I read a biography of her when I was in second grade and became fascinated not only with her accomplishments but also with the mystery surrounding her disappearance. Since I first read about her when I was seven, there has been some progress on perhaps uncovering that mystery.

WHAT HAPPENED TO AMELIA EARHART?

There are many theories about what happened to Amelia Earhart. Some people believe that she simply crashed into the Pacific Ocean on that long-ago night and died as a result of that crash. This theory is known as the "crash and sink" theory: her plane crashed and sank into the ocean.

Others have a theory that her flight was an elaborate scheme by President Franklin D. Roosevelt to have her spy on the Japanese. The problem with this theory is that not only did she not go anywhere near Japan, but her mission was hardly a secret. In fact, it was one of the most publicized events of the century!

In 1943, during World War II, several Allied airmen reported seeing Earhart working as a nurse on Guadalcanal. The person they saw probably was Merle Farland, a nurse from New Zealand, who was said to resemble the lost pilot. Many of those airmen suffered delusions brought on by malaria and other diseases, which might have fueled their belief that Amelia Earhart was their nurse.

An Australian army corporal on patrol in the jungle on the island of New Britain near Papua New Guinea in 1943 found a Pratt & Whitney aircraft engine. Earhart's plane did have a Pratt & Whitney engine, as did many planes during that time. However, Earhart had radioed that she was running out of fuel near Howland Island, so she could not have flown another 2,000 miles to New Britain.

A 1970 book claimed that Earhart survived crashing in the Pacific and was taken as a prisoner of war by the Japanese. Later, the book continued, Americans discovered her and repatriated her to New Jersey where she lived under an assumed name as Irene Bolom. However, when the real Irene Bolom read the book, she denied this, sued the author, and won.

Another rumor circulated that Amelia Earhart had been captured by the Japanese. But this one claimed she was broadcasting over the radio as one of about a dozen English-speaking women collectively known as "Tokyo Rose," who spread propaganda to disrupt the morale of the Allied troops. George Putnam investigated this rumor at the time and listened to dozens of Tokyo Rose broadcasts. He determined that none of the women was his Amelia Earhart.

Immediately after Earhart and Noonan's disappearance, the United States Navy and Earhart's mother expressed belief the flight had ended in the Phoenix Islands, about 350 miles southeast of Howland Island. In 1988, the International Group for Historical Aircraft Recovery, (TIGHAR), began an investigation of the Earhart/Noonan disappearance and since then has sent ten expeditions to the tiny coral atoll of Nikumaroro in the Phoenix Islands. They have suggested that Earhart and Noonan may have flown without further radio transmissions for two and a half hours along the line of position Earhart noted in her last transmission received at Howland, arrived at then-uninhabited Gardner Island (now Nikumaroro), landed on an extensive reef flat near the wreck of a large freighter, the SS *Norwich City*, and lived as castaways until they ultimately perished.

TIGHAR's research has produced a range of documented archaeological and anecdotal evidence supporting this hypothesis. For example, in 1940, a British colonial officer and licensed pilot named Gerald Gardiner, radioed his superiors to inform them that he had found a skeleton that was possibly a woman, along with an old-fashioned sextant box under a tree on the island's southeast corner. He was ordered to send the remains to Fiji, where British authorities took detailed measurements of the bones and concluded they were from a male about 5 feet 5 inches tall. However, in 1998 an analysis of the data by forensic anthropologists indicated the skeleton had belonged to a "tall white female of northern European ancestry," a description that fits Earhart. Unfortunately, the bones were misplaced in Fiji and have not been found.

In 2007, a TIGHAR expedition visited Nikumaroro searching for unambiguously identifiable aircraft artifacts and DNA. The group included engineers, technical experts, and others. Artifacts discovered by TIGHAR on Nikumaroro have included: improvised tools; an aluminum panel (possibly from an Electra); an oddly cut piece of clear Plexiglas the same thickness and curvature of an Electra window; a size-9 Cat's Paw heel dating from the 1930s, which resembles Earhart's footwear in world flight photos; a zipper pull that might have come from her flight suit; and a shard of a cosmetics jar that matches an Earhart-era freckle cream—but so far, nobody has found proof she used that brand.

During a 2010 expedition, the research group said it had found bones that appeared to be part of a human finger. TIGHAR believes that the evidence they have found is consistent with a castaway presence on the island. Among the most interesting are the remains of small fires with bird and fish bones; giant clams that had been opened like New England oysters; empty shells laid out as if to collect rainwater; pieces of a pocket knife; pieces of rouge and the broken mirror from a woman's compact; and prewar American bottles with melted bottoms that had once stood in a fire as if to boil drinking water. The mysterious tiny finger bone was discovered near turtle remains on the island's remote southeast end, in an area called the Seven Site, where campsite and fire features were also found.

Earhart's surviving stepson, George Putnam Jr., has expressed support for TIGHAR's research.

Another thing that excited me as I wrote *Lady Lindy* was the opportunity to write about mountain gorillas. In 2011, my sixteen-year-old son, Sam, and I visited Uganda in Africa. During the week, we taught in lower and middle schools (he taught acting and I taught writing). On the weekends, we traveled to all of the beautiful national parks around the country and saw lions, zebras, hippos, rhinos, giraffes, wildebeests, and more birds than I can document here. On our last weekend, we went to the Bwindi Impenetrable Forest, where the world's remaining mountain gorillas live. Bwindi borders the Congo, and the gorillas move freely between the countries.

Mountain gorillas are endangered. Less than 790 remain in the wild, and there are none in captivity. Many factors have contributed to their endangered status, including habitat loss, poaching, and snares meant for small game. Recently, mountain gorillas have also become the victims of neighboring human warfare.

Bwindi Impenetrable Forest has earned its name! Like the jungle where Maisie and Felix land, it has thick foliage, vines, and no paths or trails. Guides with machetes hack through the vegetation to provide paths for visitors. Other guides have rifles in case of attacks by wild animals or poachers. Sam and I visited there during the rainy season, which added to the difficult conditions.

Although we had been prepared to hike as much as seven hours into the jungle to spot the gorillas, we got lucky and saw four gorillas within about twenty minutes. They ate bark and leaves, very much like the ones that Maisie and Felix first encounter. In fact, the behavior I described in the book is what we observed. About an hour later, our guide got a walkie-talkie report that there was a silverback gorilla another ten minutes deeper in the jungle. We hiked there, and, sure enough, we found the silverback!

We had been instructed not to make eye contact with a gorilla and to keep at least ten feet away from them. But the silverback was immediately curious about *us*, and marched right over. Our guide reminded us to look at the ground, not the gorilla, and to stand very close together. I could smell him as he approached and walked right up to us, standing about a foot away and walking up and down the line we had formed.

When he got to me, he stopped for what seemed a very long time. I could hear him breathing and up close he smelled even worse! Eventually, he moved away. But just when I sighed with relief, he came up behind me and punched me hard right between the shoulder blades, sending me flying through the air. I heard Sam yell and run up to catch me, just as the gorilla started to come toward me. One of the guides picked me up and stuck me in the trunk of a dead tree, ordering everyone else to form a tight circle around me. For what seemed like forever, the silverback circled us, panting and pounding his chest, until he finally gave up. But first, he hip-checked the guide hard enough to knock him down. Only later did I learn that the silverback's nickname is "The Puncher"!

Finally, I was excited to write about women and aviation. When I got out of college, I worked as a flight attendant for TWA, the very airline that Amelia Earhart worked for! Unlike her, I did not have a desire to *fly* planes. But I did have a burning desire to travel and see the world. The first airline stewardess (that's what we were called until airlines began hiring men for the job in the 1970s), Ellen

Church, worked for what later became United Airlines. The first stewardesses had to be registered nurses, but eventually the profession became synonymous with pretty young women, even though their main role on the plane is to evacuate it during emergencies. Until the late 1960s, stewardesses could not keep their jobs if they got married. That changed slightly, allowing them to marry but forcing them to quit if they had children. By the time I became a flight attendant, the image had changed, partially because men were now doing the job but also because the role of women had changed over time. In 1978, when I started working as a TWA flight attendant, there were still only a handful of female pilots flying for commercial airlines. Today, there are over 5,200. Amelia Earhart would be proud!

Continue your adventures in
The Treasure Chest!